Cairo Connection

by

Carol Henry

Cairo Connection

Cover Art by *RJMorris*

The Wild Rose Press, Inc.
PO Box 708
Adams Basin, NY 14410-0708
Visit us at www.thewildrosepress.com

Publishing History
First Crimson Rose Edition, 2018
Print ISBN 978-1-5092-2326-8
Digital ISBN 978-1-5092-2327-5

Published in the United States of America

The drone flew directly into the ropes connecting the balloon to the basket. The jarring sent the passengers tumbling sideways in shock as the basket tilted. Megan fell against Jordan. His arms circled her protectively, catching her before she fell to her knees, or over the edge.

"What the hell!" Jordan exclaimed as he took in the situation. The mid-sized drone's spinnerets were tangled in the ropes, cutting through at a frenzied pace, and tore through several of the lines. The basket rocked, and then tilted again. The man at the controls quickly reduced the amount of flames shooting upward into the balloon and the basket took an immediate dive. Several of the ropes caught fire.

Two of the passengers on the opposite side of the basket clung precariously to the edge. *Holy Mary, Mother of God.* They were about to plummet to their deaths. The burning ropes were thrown over the side of the basket as they rapidly descended. Passengers screamed and hung on tight.

"Hang on," Jordan ordered. "Sit on my lap and tuck your head against my chest. Keep your arms and legs bent."

Megan didn't question him. If there was half a chance she'd get out of this alive, it would be due to Jordan's level-headedness.

The basket swayed, bobbed, and continued its rapid descent. Passengers were tossed about inside the basket. The couple clinging to the edge of the basket was flung overboard. Their screams echoed throughout the valley. The drone sounded like a buzz saw as it continued to cut through the ropes. Megan closed her eyes and sent up a silent prayer for the couple's safety.

Dedication

With much love to my very own high school sweetheart, my hero, best friend, and travel companion—my husband Gary. A tribute to our own great romantic Egyptian adventures.

Prologue

"The Americans did not die today." Habib El-Said inhaled tobacco from his floor-length, iridescent blue *Sheesha* pipe. He blew the smoke through his nose and mouth all the while scanning the small crowded Cairo side street coffee shop. He turned to his cohort, assured no one was within hearing range—not that those loitering close by would mind his desire to chase the Americans off the recent dig in the Luxor Valley before more antiquities were smuggled out of the country. Confident, he leaned back in the rickety folding chair and ran his hand fondly along the narrow pipe's stem. "They have been sent home, wounded and empty handed. A warning to others."

"What about Henry Kaine?" His friend, Salah Delagad, lifted his small cup filled with rich, dark coffee, and sipped before continuing. "Did you spare his life, as I asked?" He held the tiny saucer in his left hand while he drank from the miniature cup.

"A shame, but yes," Habib confirmed. "For now, Henry Kaine is safe. I promise you, if he does not let the Egyptian Antiquities Ministry take charge of the most recent finds, I cannot guarantee his safety. You understand?" Habib eyed Salah Delagad as he caressed the rubber smoke hose attached to the bubbling water pipe, and inhaled, the smoke circling his head this time.

"Of course. What about the Brits?" Salah's dark eyebrows rose into his thick, matted hair sticking out from under his white turban.

"Only five more Brit students are on site. Unless they have been scared off by this minor 'accident'." Habib continued to puff from his water pipe, savoring the fragrant scent of the citric flavored tobacco. "Ah, but the British are much more 'stiff-upper-lip' and aren't so easily shaken. Besides, I doubt they are the ones funneling our valuable finds to New York."

"I know you want the lead on this one—keep relics in Egypt where they belong," Salah said. "Do not be over zealous in your task—we do not want pandemonium to erupt such as what happened during the 2011 Cairo riots. Let's keep it simple and clean, and everything will remain intact."

"The riots were altogether a different occasion, my friend. Yet, you have my word," Habib assured him.

"We do not want more antiquities destroyed or to disappear like what happened in the Cairo Museum."

"Agreed." Ahhh, his friend had a kind heart. It was a good thing he had other men on his payroll if this one failed. "When do you fly back to Luxor, Salah?"

"Not for three days. I will first attend the Cairo International Conference on Agriculture."

"I understand one of Mr. Kaine's sons is arriving in Cairo for the Conference. He could be the connection we need to prove Henry Kaine's duplicity. Keep me informed of his movements while he is here, especially where his father is concerned. This son will travel the regions to visit grower's operations and I want to know where he goes, who he talks to, and if he visits his father. He has very close ties to his father and we do not need another American—a Kaine—interfering with Egypt's business and walking off with our prized treasures. You understand?"

"Of course. I will arrange for someone to 'tail' him as soon as he arrives in Cairo."

"Use Omar Nagid. Have him report directly to me if he learns anything," Habib instructed. "I will see you in Luxor. Until then, do not contact me unless it is of dire importance."

Habib El-Said remained puffing on his pipe as Salah Delagad finished his coffee, placed his cup and saucer on the small wooden table, rose, and ambled down the narrow street, where he disappeared into the crowded, back street community. As soon as Habib finished his smoke, he would put a tail on his friend. Salah Delagad was altogether too friendly with the Americans—and Henry Kaine—to be trustworthy.

Chapter One

What the hell was Jordan Kaine doing standing in front of her desk at Wild and Wonderful Corporation headquarters? His tall, rugged, and handsome as all get out good looks had Megan Holloway catching her breath, swallowing hard, wanting to check her makeup, and make sure her hair was in place.

"Professor Kaine. What can I do for you?" Megan had all to do not to swallow her tongue. She nervously flicked her long, straight auburn hair behind her ears, gulped, and in an attempt to sound professional, said, "I'm afraid Miss Mapes isn't available. She's in France at the moment."

Good heavens, the smile he gave her lit up the man's dreamy blue-gray eyes—deeper than the sea, and as sparkly as if the sun was shining on pulsing waves. She'd had a secret crush on him four years ago in college—how stereotypical of her—falling for her college professor. She hadn't seen him since and had been ever so thankful that he'd never had an inkling of her infatuation. After all, he'd been engaged to be married at the time. She checked his left hand and found no ring. Either the wedding never took place, or the marriage didn't last. Or he was one of those who enjoyed an open relationship-type marriage.

"I'm aware Helen is still in France, Miss Holloway. My cousin asked me to fill in for her specifically to handle the Egyptian account. We're collaborating on a contract with the Egyptian Ministry of Agriculture."

So, he was her temporary boss while Helen Mapes was in France. There had been mention of a relative filling in for Helen, but Megan hadn't yet been told who had taken her place. Thankfully she wasn't familiar with the Egyptian account, so she wouldn't have to work closely with Professor Jordan Kaine. She'd only worked for Wild and Wonderful Corporation a few months. It was a well-respected grass-roots organization and had gained a stellar reputation for helping to obtain contracts internationally. Whether to improve their economy, make sure other companies or institutions weren't overstepping environmental standards, as well as endangering people, flora, and fauna in the wild, Helen Mapes had built the business into a much sought after enterprise in New York's Finger Lakes Region. Closer to the University and Professor Kaine's place of employment then she was suddenly comfortable with.

Again, she wondered what part Professor Kaine played in regards to the Egyptian account.

"Can I help you with something?"

"Yes. I'm sorry this is such short notice, but I just spoke to Helen earlier today. She instructed me to request you accompany me to Cairo this Friday."

What! Cairo! OMG! Was he serious? Cairo? Friday? Her?

Megan took a deep breath, removed her hands from the keyboard, pushed her chair away from the monitor, and stood to face her temporary boss.

"Are you sure she requested me? I haven't been here long enough to be sent out on such an important assignment. What about Darla Slidell? She's been here much longer. I'm sure Darla is better qualified." There was no way Megan was prepared to spend any amount of time working alongside Jordan Kaine. He was more handsome now than he had been four years ago.

"Not an option. Helen recommended your excellent organizational and social skills for this assignment, not to mention your background in horticulture. I assume you do have a passport."

"Yes. It was one of the requirements for the job." Not that she thought she'd ever have an opportunity or need to use it. When she had interviewed for the position, Helen insisted she obtain a passport ASAP. Other than what Helen had gleaned from her résumé and a brief interview before hiring her, her boss didn't know her from Adam—or Eve. Within a week of being hired, Helen had flown off to France, trusting her to do her job unsupervised. If Helen only knew the position she had unknowingly put her in by requesting her to accompany Jordan Kaine on this trip, she might have thought twice about choosing her. And it didn't help that her job at Wild and Wonderful was tenuous—her three-month probationary period was up in two weeks. If she refused to go on this assignment with Jordan Kaine, would she be unemployed by the end of the day?

"Good to know you're prepared. Make sure your shots are up to date. We leave Friday evening. I've ordered airport limo service to pick you up at five. Pack light."

Was he kidding? Friday? Shots? What shots? Oh, crap. Only three days to prepare for a trip that was going to take her half way around the world. Some people might be ecstatic to learn they were about to embark on a trip of a lifetime—she wasn't convinced she was one of them. Who wouldn't like to explore Egypt—the cradle of civilization? But right now, she had responsibilities at home. Her mother was just settling into a temporary care rehabilitation facility. She depended on Megan to make sure her every need was met—financially, as well. Being gone for any length of time was going to be hard on her mother and more than likely set the whole healing process back. If she lost her job, she wouldn't have the funds to pay for the upscale facility.

Megan stifled the deep sigh she longed to emit. Instead, she lowered her eyes for a brief moment, and then looked back up at Jordan Kaine's chin. "How long will we be in Egypt?"

"At least a week. Maybe longer. Hard to say. We'll be visiting several of the fields, so pack appropriately. Take the rest of the day off and deal with any situation that needs your personal attention."

Was he kidding? Three days to get her affairs in order? What affairs? He talked as if she wasn't coming back. And get shots, pack, and make sure her mother was going to be okay during her absence wasn't something she could simply wave a magic wand and it would be done. And, what about her responsibilities in the office? Helen was waiting for those reports on France.

"I have reports due on the French files on Burgundy and Provence for Helen's clients in Paris."

"Helen emailed me the other day and said you can give the files to Miss Slidell. She's familiar with the project."

He left her standing behind her desk, his hands in his pants pockets as he headed out the door. She was about to sit down when Jordan Kaine stopped, rested his left hand on the doorframe, and glanced over his shoulder. His pinched lips and lowered eyebrows did nothing to take away from his tall, dark, handsome features. The guy had a muscular physique—evident beneath the snug twill navy shirt that brought out the blue in his eyes. The pose alone was nothing short of model material. She focused on his face and caught her breath at his brooding expression. Now what?

"The company will cover any expenses you incur in regards to this assignment—within reason. Check with Mr. Lear in accounting. He'll issue you an advance. Pick it up on your way out. Keep all your receipts."

"You should know that I haven't worked on the Cairo conference project," she called as he headed down the hall. "I'm not prepared." She raised her voice hoping he could still hear. "Do you have a copy of the file I can study?"

"No time," his voice echoed down the hall, his footsteps tapping between his words as he made his way down the corridor. "I'll fill you in on the plane."

A door shut. Silence descended and echoed throughout her office space. She was in the Twilight Zone. Had Professor Kaine just demanded she go to Egypt? With him? Oh, hell no! She'd never been outside New York State, let alone stepped inside a jet.

She was caught between excitement at traveling to Egypt, concern that she wasn't prepared for the project Helen had been working on, and anxiety over leaving her mother's side. She was wedged between the proverbial rock and a hard place. She needed this job. The financial responsibility of her mother's care rested solely on her shoulders, and the next payment was due the end of the month. How was she going to explain to her mother she wouldn't be able to visit every day? Her mother wasn't going to understand how important it was that she travel to Egypt in order to keep this job. The pay was too good to pass up, especially with a bonus at the end of the probationary period. It would go a long way to continue to care for her mother, as well as maintain her own small apartment.

Megan plunked down in her black office chair—it rolled backward and hit the long green credenza behind her desk with a bang. Darn it, she needed this job. This meant she needed to perform well enough to receive a good evaluation at the end of the month. If she refused to go to Egypt with Professor Kaine, her evaluation, and her job, would be as good as gone.

She swung around, faced the monitor, put her hands on the keyboard to start a list of things to do, shopping items, and things to pack. And froze. Having never flown before, or been out of the country, she didn't have a single clue how to prepare for such a trip. And on such short notice. Professor Kaine didn't mention what airline they'd be on, so she had no inkling what their requirements were. She selected the phonebook from the shelf above the monitor and looked up the local airport's number. After a quick call, she was armed with various internet sites that she was assured would give her the much needed travel information.

She keyed in the Transportation Security Administration site on the computer and scrolled down their list. She didn't plan to transport any weapons, tools, explosives, or sporting goods. As for sharp items in her carry-on, she'd have to remove her nail file and replace it with an emery board. Finding nothing else she needed to add to her list, she scrolled to the side bar and read up on the 'liquid' rule, made notes, and moved on. She typed 'luggage' on her list, added 'check medical records,' and chewed on the inside of her cheek. What was she going to pack in the luggage? Her closet wasn't exactly lined with lightweight clothing. Central New York's weather didn't rival Egypt's arid desert conditions. And where was she going to buy such clothing here in the middle of winter? On such short notice? She needed to talk to someone. And right now, the only person she could think of, who might have some tips to share, was her best friend from high school, Lindsey Weeks.

Megan hit print, and while she waited for the list to spit out, she made sure her office was secure for a possible two-week absence. She slipped into her knee-length black leather boots, grabbed her purse, her shoe bag, coat, and the list from the printer, shut everything off, and then made her way to Darla's office to deliver the files on France.

"Sorry to bother you, Darla," Megan said after giving a perfunctory knock on the doorframe and entering the assistant's office. "I've been assured Professor Kaine has filled you in about the Egypt trip."

She stood in front of Darla's disorganized desk. Her coat draped over her arm, she handed the file to her co-worker. When Darla didn't take the report, Megan scanned the chaos that was Darla's immediate surroundings, and decided to place it in the center of the desk.

Despite the cluttered office, Darla was a picture of unblemished beauty—her well-defined makeup and slim figure were nothing short of perfection. Her flawlessly styled bleach blonde head bobbled as if looking for something important as she tapped her manicured, blood-red polished fingernails against the desk. She reached for a handful of loose sheets, shuffled them together on the desk, then stapled them and placed them in a folder before setting it next to another pile on the opposite corner. She folded her hands on top of the desk, and the folder Megan had just placed in front of her, and only then acknowledged Megan's presence.

Megan sighed. Even if she wanted to, there was no competing with Darla's good looks and fashion sense.

"Yes, well, I do know the files backward and forward in regards to the conference in Cairo. I also know you don't." Darla pursed her dark red lips that identically matched her nails and raised her perfectly tweezed eyebrows.

If looks could kill!

Darla didn't refer to the Paris files. If Megan wanted to keep this job, she needed to make nice with the others in the office. That meant Darla. She'd be working with Darla when she returned from Egypt. Jordan Kaine and Helen obviously had no idea the position they'd put her in.

"I do understand, and I was as surprised as you," Megan attempted to appease the obviously resentful girl. "You're better informed than I am about the project. In fact, if you want to take it up with Professor Kaine, I'm okay with you taking my place."

Darla's expression became wary. Like an owl, her head rotated sideways as she peered at Megan from the corner of her eyes. Or was it a sly look? Obviously, it had been a mistake to stop by Darla's office. She should have emailed the files instead or placed the documentation in the assistant's mailbox. Deciding not to prolong the encounter with Darla any longer than necessary, Megan referred back to the France project, and pointed at the folder under Darla's hands.

"All the information I've organized for the Paris project is in that file."

"Yes, Jordan filled me in on the France project earlier today. I'll take care of it for Jordan while he's gone."

The way Darla said 'Jordan' instead of referring to Helen, in her saccharine-sweet voice spoke volumes—indicating her keen interest in Jordan Kaine. Clearly, she had hoped to accompany him on this assignment. Those daggers coming from Darla's eyes made it clear she wasn't happy Megan was the lucky one chosen for the trip. Megan wasn't exactly happy about being the chosen one either.

"I'm sorry, Darla. My hands are tied. Could you give me a few tips on what to expect at these conferences?"

"I'm not a tour director. I've never been to Egypt."

Yep, the woman was envious, and a tad bit jealous.

"Sorry, Darla, I did suggest he ask you to go to Egypt instead of me."

"You did?" Her eyebrows shot through her hairline, her eyeballs almost popping out of her head. The frown disappeared, transforming her face so fast, Megan stepped back as if the woman was possessed.

"Of course. I know you're better informed on the project, and better qualified as far as travel goes. I don't know what they were thinking." She had a feeling she did know—Darla was more than obviously smitten with their new temporary boss—her reputation with men wasn't exactly a secret. Little did Darla know that after the incident Jordan Kaine had gone through at the university several years ago, his heart was locked up tighter than the location of the Holy Grail.

****

Megan Holloway was right. What the hell was he thinking? He should have insisted Darla Slidell go to Egypt instead. Helen hadn't given him a choice. It was obvious from the two days he'd filled in for Helen that Darla already had her sights set on him. He knew her kind and wasn't interested. He needed to keep the woman at a distance. If she were to accompany him, he would be too busy evading her advances and unable to concentrate on the conference and securing the contract with the Egyptian Ministry of Agriculture.

He shook his head as he exited the building and headed to the car park. Darla's interest in him had nothing to do with love. She was after that next rung up the ladder—assuming his connection to Helen was her ticket to the top. He'd been a near victim to that state of affairs many times at the university—had almost gotten caught up in a lawsuit. Young girls thinking they could improve their grades by having sex with their professors was nothing new. He'd been warned, and he had heeded those warnings. It had saved his ass more than once. Having to deal with disgruntled students was always painful, especially when there was at least one new case each semester. A new cluster of hot, sexy girls let loose from their families for the first time, and the fact that they didn't know how to handle their raging hormones didn't help.

Sure he'd been tempted. What single, hot blooded male wouldn't be? There had been the occasional student who had him taking nightly cold showers. He had to admit Megan Holloway had been one of them. Granted, she had never 'come on to him'—maybe that was one of the things that had intrigued him about her in the first place. But he had been engaged to Natalie. Regardless, he wasn't about to get involved with a student. *Ever!*

Megan hadn't been one of 'those girls' four years ago when all hell had broken loose with Whitney Nash's accusations. Megan Holloway had been a beautiful young lady back then and was even more so now. Just standing in front of her desk, staring into those deep green emerald eyes that seemed to look right through him had his heart standing still and his tongue tied. Her long auburn hair as she brushed it behind her ears only accentuated those eyes, and her small, perfect nose. He hadn't been able to keep his eyes off her lush lips as she talked.

It didn't matter how hard he'd tried to talk Helen out of sending Megan with him on this trip. Helen had been adamant—impressed with Megan's excellent organizational skills, as well as her background in horticulture.

Dammit. Rumor mills thrived in academic circles. Hopefully, she wouldn't remember the incident with Whitney, and hold it against him. And dredge up the past.

He was up for tenure.

The cold December wind blowing off Cayuga Lake hit him full force the minute he stepped out of the building. He tugged his jacket tighter, shoved his hands in his pockets, and jogged to his vehicle through the light dusting of snow. He slid behind the wheel of his old Chevy extended cab truck, stretched his leg toward the brake pedal, and turned the key in the ignition. The truck might be old, but it was in superb running condition. He'd needed to keep it running smoothly since his extension responsibilities at the university had him traveling around New York State visiting many of the growers. Today, however, he was headed back to the university to meet with Greg Sampson, his co-worker, who was also going to Cairo to present a paper on their recent joint research project. The committee was working in conjunction with Wild and Wonderful, and thanks to Helen, Jordan was the liaison between the two.

Jordan took a deep breath and blew it out. Dammit. He couldn't get Megan's look of panic out of his head. Helen better be right about her being an asset to the company. From her reaction and lack of international travel, she was already a liability. He ran his hands down his upper pant legs as he checked the traffic pattern, then gripped the steering wheel, and eased out of the parking lot into the street. He drove up the hill toward the university. Taking a sabbatical so he could step in to help his cousin at Wild and Wonderful Corporation was bad enough, but traipsing off to Cairo to attend the conference on Sustainable Horticulture Production Practices, and Water Management along the Nile with Megan Holloway at his side was going to be more stressful than he'd anticipated. Not to mention checking in with his father and brother on their current archeological dig while he was in Luxor.

Tenure better be worth it.

Chapter Two

"Egypt! You're going to Egypt?" Megan's mother grabbed her chest and leaned against the pillow. "What am I going to do without you?"

Tears rolled down her mother's pale cheeks. Megan reached over, snatched a tissue from the night stand next to the bed, and wiped her mother's tears.

"You'll be okay, Mom. I'll only be gone a few days. You're in good hands here at River Cove, and the doctors assure me you've been improving every day."

Megan knew her mother would be upset when she told her about the trip. She'd prepared herself for the worst and had anticipated her mother laying on the guilt—and the tears. Megan's heart ached as it was. She didn't need the extra added guilt before she'd even packed. She understood her mother's trepidation. To be fair, her mother had been through a lot lately. Her second husband had been killed in an auto accident while they were on their way to their time-share in Florida for the winter. After her surgery for a broken hip and crushed ankle, her mother had learned of her husband's death. In a state of shock and grief, she had suffered a TIA—a mini stroke, leaving the left side of her body partially paralyzed.

Megan bent over, kissed her mother's forehead, and cradled her thin, cold hands between her own hands.

"I won't be gone forever. It's only for a week at most. They're taking excellent care of you here. I'll make sure Mrs. Williams has my contact information in case she needs to get in touch."

"I'm not going to be around forever, you know. I could have another stroke while you're traipsing all over Egypt."

"I understand how hard this is for you, Mom. I'll worry about you every day, but I need this job. It's not a vacation—it's a job. If I refuse to go, I'll get a bad evaluation and be let go."

"Posh, honey, you don't need this job. With your education, you can find another one." Her mother hiccupped, and took a deep breath, slid her hands out from Megan's and waved them in the air. "Besides, once the insurance snafu is settled from the accident, these expenses will be covered."

Had her mother's second husband not left his estate and money to his first wife—a shock, to say the least—the fees for the reconstruction home, and an apartment for the two of them wouldn't be an issue. The facility wasn't waiting for the insurance company to process the claim. They wanted their money up front and on a monthly basis. Having landed this job with Wild and Wonderful three months ago had been a godsend. Megan couldn't afford to mess up.

Her mother slid her thin, bony fingers under the covers, drawing the sheet up around her neck. "It's cold in here. Tell them to turn up the heat."

"I'll get you another blanket, as well."

Her mother sighed, turned her head into the plush pillow, and groaned in pain.

"Do you need more pain medication? Can I get you anything else?"

Her mother's eyes closed.

Guilt settled in—again. Her mother hadn't gotten what she wanted so she was heaping on the guilt. Megan bit her lower lip, closed her eyes, and prayed her mother wouldn't prove more difficult while she was in Egypt.

"I'll be in touch as often as possible while I'm away. I have to go for now. I have things to do to get ready for this trip. I'll see you later. Try to get some rest." She kissed her mother's forehead, heard another deep sigh, and saw the tears leak from beneath long lashes resting on pasty pale cheeks.

Megan's heart thumped in her chest, and she hung her head. She had to leave before her own tears started to flow. She shut the door to her mother's private room behind her and leaned against the wall in the hallway. She shook her head, the responsibility heavy, her heart so bogged down with guilt she was tempted to sit on the floor and sob. But it would get her nowhere. She loved her mother, and wasn't looking forward to leaving her behind, despite knowing she was in good hands. Her mother didn't have to remind her she might suffer another stroke. She was aware of the possibilities. She prayed her going away wouldn't cause her mother unnecessary stress and another stroke.

"Miss Holloway." Mrs. Williams appeared around the corner at the end of the corridor, a worried frown on her round, rosy face, her brows raised into her white hairline. "Is Nettie okay? Does she need something? Should I call for help?"

"Mom is a bit cold. I told her I'd see about getting another blanket. But I'm glad you're here. I was about to look for you. I need to discuss a situation that has developed this morning." Megan stepped away from the wall and brushed the stray hairs around her ears and fixed her purse strap over her shoulder. "I'm afraid I've upset her."

"I'll have someone check in on her STAT. Come. Let's go to my office. I'll have one of the aides get your mother a warmed blanket. Can I get you a coffee?"

"Thanks, no. I'm okay."

Mrs. Williams withdrew a small black phone from her paisley print scrubs, keyed in a number, and left a message for one of the aides as they walked down the hallway toward the elevator. Megan followed the nurse into the elevator, then to Mrs. Williams' office.

"Make yourself comfortable, my dear." The nurse indicated the chair in front of her desk.

Megan sat in the hard, straight-back chair while Mrs. Williams walked behind her desk and sat facing her. The woman's smile was indicative of a caring "I'm here for you" professional. Megan could see the fatigue in the woman's eyes. The woman needed a vacation from dealing with too many patients like her mother. Too bad Megan couldn't send her to Egypt in her place.

"Now, what can I do for you?"

"I'm sorry to bother you with this, Mrs. Williams, and I know this is short notice, but I'm about to go out of the country on assignment. I'm afraid my mother is a bit upset because I won't be able to visit her every day. I've assured her she is in good hands, and that I'll be a phone call away should the need arise. I leave this Friday and will most likely be gone for a week—or two, at most. I know the payment for her care is due the first of the month, but I might be a day or two late."

"I'm glad you came to me."

"River Cove did come highly recommended, and I've been very pleased with her care. I know she can be difficult at times. I appreciate all you've done to help ease her pain since her accident and loss of her husband."

"Thank you, we do care for our patients. It's good to hear you're satisfied with her care. I fear she's harder on you than she is on us. Patients in her situation often tend to take it out on their loved ones. They feel neglected, lonely, especially when they're in pain and have lost a loved one. The healing process can be a long one. Now, we can certainly work around your schedule. As for the payment, if you find it difficult, and are going to be later than anticipated, give me a call. But please be aware there is a long waiting list for rooms."

Megan didn't need to be reminded that she was about to put a strain on her mother's healing by leaving her neglected and lonely. She was also aware of the waiting list—her mother had had to wait two weeks before her number came up to be admitted. In the meantime, the hospital bills had piled up. Being in this facility had only increased the financial burden.

"I'll be in contact as often as possible."

"Always helpful. I hope your assignment goes well."

Megan sighed. Her guilt slightly eased. Next step? Talk to her friend Lindsey. See if she had any information on traveling to Egypt. As a world travel writer, Lindsey was sure to have a few tips on how to dress, what to pack, and how to handle her fear of flying. However, she wasn't sure Lindsey would have any advice about her traveling with the handsome Professor Kaine. He might be a top notch professor from a major university, but the man had a body that suggested he did more than visit growers, sit behind a desk, lecture behind a podium, or scribble on a chalk board—the man's body was in excellent condition. Vitality oozed from his every pore. He was a walking seduction. She didn't even want to dwell on those full, kissable lips, the dimple in his right cheek when he smiled, his sable hair, the kind you just wanted to run your fingers through.

She'd had a crush on him when she had registered for his class four years ago, but then, so did all the other girls in his class. He'd been off limits, projecting a cold, professional demeanor that shouted hands off! There had been one incident with a girl in her dorm, Whitney Nash. After the dust settled, Whitney had transferred to another university and Megan had put it out of her mind. Megan had moved on, concentrated on her own classes, and earned her degree.

But, holy crap, she'd be flying to Cairo with him in a matter of days. She'd be sitting next to him in a jet for hours—at night. Sleeping next to him on a plane. God forbid she fell asleep and accidently leaned her head against his shoulder. Her face prickled and warmed just thinking about the possibility. Man, was she in trouble.

She should start looking for another job immediately.

****

"So? Jordon Kaine? How did this come about?" Lindsey asked.

Her friend's fair skin and light freckles dotting along her cheeks complemented her long Irish-red ponytail and her petite and effervescent personality. Her ponytail wiggled down her back as she took cups down from the cupboard. She inserted a pod in the coffee maker, placed a cup on the drip tray, and pressed the button. The hiss of water running through the machine filled the small, compact kitchenette, and the aroma of fresh coffee calmed Megan's tension. *Hazelnut—yes!*

"I thought he was some hunky professor at the university you had a crush on years ago. What's he doing at Wild and Wonderful? And taking you to Cairo with him? Which you will simply love, by the way. You must be sure to see the Sphinx and the Pyramids. Oh, and Luxor and the Nile. How romantic." Her friend from high school sighed, clasped her hands in front of her generous chest as if she were about to swoon like a Victorian virgin.

"Hold on a minute. This is not a romantic vacation. As much as I'm starting to get excited about traveling to Egypt, I'm not eager to go with Professor Kaine."

Lindsey gave her the familiar, disbelieving eye-roll she was so capable of giving on more than one occasion, and handed Megan the first cup of coffee, steam rising. Megan added a heaping teaspoon of sugar, a liberal amount of half and half, and took a sip. It warmed her insides and immediately soothed her frayed nerves. Meanwhile, Lindsey prepared her own vanilla cream coffee, plunked in the chair across from Megan, and rested her elbows on the table, cup in hand.

"Really, Lindsey, you know I've never stepped foot on a jet. What am I going to do?"

"Jet, schmet. You'll be fine. I'm talking about *THE* Jordan Kaine. Lady Killer Kaine." She paused and took a tentative sip from her mug. "Now's your chance— you're no longer one of his students. I say go for it. Live a little. Have fun. Have a fling. Why, have sex for a change."

"*Lindsey!*"

"Oh, Megan. Lighten up." Lindsey set her cup on the table. "It's the 21st Century, for crying out loud. And I'm sure he's been around the proverbial barn a few times. You can't judge every man based on Rick's actions. Just because Rick didn't love you enough to stick it out to help take care of you and your mother in your hour of need, doesn't mean every man is as shallow."

"I repeat. This is not a vacation—romantic or otherwise. And Rick has nothing to do with this."

"Good to hear. So live a little."

"I only came to you for advice on what to pack, and what to expect as far as the Egyptian culture, not advice on my love life—or lack of a love life. And, to see if you would keep an eye on Abigail for me while I'm gone. That is, unless you're going to be off traveling somewhere exotic while I'm away."

"Not for another couple of months. And yes, that big ole girl is welcome here anytime. Make sure you have enough food and her favorite doggie dish and snacks."

"Done. Thanks. I don't know what I would have done if you weren't able to watch Mom's dog. I can't afford a kennel on my salary—not with Mom's bills coming in. I'll drop Abby off Friday morning. I leave Friday evening."

"How is your mom?"

"Improving, although slowly. The doctor says she's fine. The risk of another stroke is low."

"That must be a huge relief for you. I'm so glad she's going to be all right. I just love your mom to pieces. I'm sure it's hard on her, not being able to get out of bed on her own. She was such an active person before the accident."

"I know it's hard on her. I'm doing all I can to make sure she has the best care and attention she needs." Megan lifted her cup, swirled the coffee, and then took a full sip before looking back at her friend. "I hate to ask, Lindsey, but I wondered if you would mind stopping by to visit Mom on occasion. Your friendship might relieve her mind and lift her spirits while I'm gone. Plus, it will ease some of the guilt she's heaped on me. Having someone she loves, and loves her, stopping by to visit while I'm away will help me, as well as my mom, a lot. I'll call as often as I can."

"I'll do it in a heartbeat." Lindsey reached across the table and clasped Megan's hand, and gave it a snug squeeze. "Count on it. But you have to do me a favor in return."

Lindsey's reassuring touch brought tears to Megan's eyes. She had all to do to form words. "Yeah? Like what?"

"I want a blow by blow report of your travels with Lady Killer Kaine when you return."

Megan threw her head back and laughed. "There will be nothing to report. So I'm safe in that respect. Now, are you going to give me some travel tips I can use, or not?"

Lindsey's lopsided grin indicated she was serious and would pounce on Megan the minute she returned from Egypt.

"Okay. Okay," Lindsay said. "Tip number one—relax. You'll be fine. You mother will be fine." Lindsey stretched her hand across the table and patted Megan's hand again, this time as if she was a little child who needed reassuring. Which, she did.

"Easy for you to say. You're a natural at this travel stuff. I don't know how you do it—jetting all over the world on your own. Going to the back-of-beyond to get that exclusive story and photo shoots."

"Guess I'm more curious about what's out there than worry about what I have to do to get my story."

"You don't have a worry bone in your body. Besides not knowing anything about traveling to Egypt, this is the first conference for Wild and Wonderful I've attended, and I don't know what's really expected of me—my responsibilities. I'd at least like to be prepared for the everyday travel stuff that you're so good at."

"What? You don't know what your duties will be? Then why are you the one going?"

"Good question. I wish I knew. I told Professor Kaine he should take Darla instead. He said Helen recommended me. I know I'm going to screw this up big time. I'll be out of a job by the end of the month, if not before this trip is over. My probationary period is up in two weeks. If I do anything to make him unhappy with my 'excellent organizational skills' as he said Helen stated, then I'm out of a job."

"At least you'll get an all-expense paid trip out of it—and a new wardrobe. Tip Two—let's go shopping. We can start at Victoria's Secret."

"No! Not Victoria's Secret. I'll be better off shopping on my own. Again, I'm not in the market to seduce anyone, let alone Jordan Kaine."

"Liar. You can't afford not to let me go shopping with you. I'll pick you up tomorrow morning at 9:45—stores open at 10:00."

Chapter Three

Jordan almost didn't recognize Megan Holloway as she entered the airport terminal. She'd cut her beautiful long auburn hair—short. Real short. She looked like a sixteen-year old pixie. A sexy, petite pixie. The teal cape wrapped around her body clear to her knees did little to erase the vision of her delectable curves hidden beneath. The beige tights and ankle length hiking boots on her small feet were a far cry from the heels she'd worn at the office. And for some reason, the brogans made her look even sexier. God help him. Taking her along on this assignment was a mistake looking for a place to happen.

Nope. Wasn't going there. She might be a beautiful woman and had done well in his class—and overall, managing a 4.0 GPA when she graduated, he'd noted—but she was as off limits now as she had been back in his class. Besides, he needed to keep his mind focused on the assignment to land that contract. And tenure.

She looked lost already, her face pale beneath her makeup, which he hadn't noticed her wearing at the office. One would think she'd never been in an airport terminal before the way she stopped and scanned the place. He needed to have a word with Helen. He let out a deep sigh, shook his head, and headed her way.

"Miss Holloway, over here." He waved his arms in the air until he got her attention.

She spotted him, stood for a moment, and then slowly made her way toward him, dragging her luggage behind with one hand, the other clutching her shoulder bag. And oh, Lord, her perfect white teeth were biting her full, red lower lip as if she was headed to the guillotine. His insides churned. He gave himself a mental shake as if his mother was standing in front of him chastising him for having done something naughty. Okay. Point taken. Meghan Holloway had nothing to worry about from him—he had a job to do, and it didn't involve becoming involved with her. Or anyone else, for that matter. He'd learned his lesson long ago.

"I have your tickets. Give me your passport. We'll check in, go through security, and find our gate." He extended his hand, palm up.

"I've never flown before." Her hand shook as she placed her passport in his open hand.

Great. Helen had assigned a travel novice to the project.

"Follow my lead. I'll get you through this."

He heard her deep sigh. The only plus so far was that she had the mandatory one piece carry-on luggage and a medium sized check-in bag. Not the multiple, overweight luggage most women checked through, expected the company to cover the extra expense, and someone else to lug around.

Chalk one up for Miss Holloway.

With any luck, she wouldn't have a ton of non-carry-on items hidden in her purse.

"You don't happen to have any large bottles of liquid, sharp items, or…"

"I may not have flown before, Professor Kaine…"

"Jordan. Might as well use my given name, we're going to be in each other's company all week."

"Jordan…, doesn't mean I wasn't smart enough to check with the airlines, TSA, and a well-traveled friend of mine. I assure you, I won't get pulled over for illegal possession of anything and embarrass you or the company."

The lady had a spark to her that made his insides smile. Perhaps she wasn't the quiet little 'mouse' he'd originally thought. *One more point in her favor.*

"Glad to hear it," he said. "As soon as we get to our gate, we can get a drink and settle in before the flight."

"I've taken a Dramamine. I don't think I should be drinking."

"A cup of tea, then?" He was beginning to feel like a yo-yo, with her yanking the string. She might not be able to have any alcohol, but he damn sure needed a drink.

"Perhaps you could start filling me in on the project."

Right. She didn't know a thing about the project, as well as traveling. Shit. That alone just cancelled all the good points he was handing out in her favor.

"We'll have plenty of time later. Right now, you need to relax and get the first leg of our trip behind us. It's a short flight to JFK. Once you see how smooth going this portion of the trip is, you'll wonder why you never flew before. After our connecting flight lifts off for Cairo, I'll fill you in—we'll have plenty of time then—it's approximately a ten-hour flight."

****

Megan's mind latched on to the fact that she would be sitting next to Jordan for ten hours as they flew across the vast ocean after leaving JFK and land behind. She followed Jordan in a daze to their departure gate where he then led her to a small café and ordered her a cup of tea and a pastry from the small bakery. Instead of getting the 'drink' he said he needed, she was surprised to see that he also ordered tea. They didn't have much time to linger before their flight was called. Megan followed Jordan's every step as they walked on to the flight line toward the small commuter plane waiting to carry them to JFK. Her stomach lurched as she approached the steep steps leading to the body of the turbo prop.

"Follow me. I'll see we get to our assigned seats." Jordan took her hand-luggage and proceeded to climb the stairway.

Once they boarded, they were shown to the front section of the plane, and their seats. Jordan stowed their carry-on luggage in the overhead and gave her the option of the window seat. She declined. No way was she going to look out the miniscule window and see nothing but air and floating clouds wiz by. She waited for him to sit, then did the same.

Fifteen minutes later, the plane backed up, turned, and taxied down the runway. Megan gripped the arms of her seat as they prepared to pull up the wheels for lift off. The centrifugal force had her entire body pressed against the back of the seat as they gained altitude. Her breath stuck in her chest. Her mouth went dry. She couldn't move. She shut her eyes against the dizziness. A lump that felt like the size of a bowling ball and just as heavy, stuck in her throat. A large warm hand covered hers. She opened her eyes and sucked in as much air as her lungs could handle. Jordan Kaine looked at her as if he didn't know what to do with her—as if she was a liability he didn't want to deal with. But his eyes—the effect of those beautiful dreamy bedroom eyes hit her midsection. She was stuck in an alternate universe and didn't know how to transfer back to reality. He squeezed her hand—his touch grounding her. She shut her eyes and did a quick prayer heavenward.

"Relax. We're airborne and everything is okay." His words floated around her addled brain, her head metaphorically and literally in the clouds. "You'll be okay. Breathe. Take a couple deep breaths. In fact, they've turned off the seatbelt sign. If you need to put your head down, go ahead."

She followed his instructions and felt much better as her head dangled between her knees. The dizziness abated. She sat back, not meeting his eyes.

"Thanks. I'm okay now." She was a complete idiot. It didn't help that he appeared uncomfortable at having to take care of such a novice. He sat back in his own seat and turned toward the window. He groaned as he rubbed his hand over his face, through his hair, and then gripped the seat's arm rest.

OMG! Her job was in jeopardy already?

She readjusted her seatbelt and made sure it was secure regardless of the seatbelt light being turned off. Just when she was starting to relax, the plane hit a deep air pocket. The plane bounced, dipped, bounced back up, shook, and then leveled out. The tea and cake she had consumed back at the Ithaca airport was working its way up into the back of her throat threatening to embarrass her by making an unwanted appearance. She swallowed, laid her head against the headrest, shut her eyes, and pretended to doze. If Jordan noticed, she wasn't aware. By the time they reached JFK and disembarked, Megan wondered how she was ever going to survive the ten-hour flight to Egypt.

Once again Megan followed Jordan every step of the way through JFK Airport. The AirTran transported them to their connecting flight, and then they passed through check-in. Thankfully he was a gentleman and assisted her, making the transition a smooth one. The wait at the gate to board the 747 was minimal. However, stepping from the ramp onto the jet had her stomach dropping clear to her toes despite the Dramamine. Maybe she needed another dose to get her through the night. But she knew better. She had to remain alert to review the files with Jordan before they landed in Egypt.

Surprised to find they were seated in the first class section where there was a minimum of seats but plenty of leg room, Megan let out a deep breath and relaxed. The seats were comfy, plush, and reclined to a sleeping position. Fluffy pillows in pristine pillowcases, warm blankets, and cabin attendants were at the ready. She just might get some sleep on this flight after all. Although sitting next to Jordan Kaine for ten hours— elbow to elbow, knee to knee—she wasn't so certain sleep would be possible.

Once seated, Megan on the inside, she was relieved when Jordan settled in and once again opened his laptop and acted as if she didn't exist while they waited for the plane to finish boarding and prepare for take-off. She sat back in her comfortable seat, adjusted everything within reach, and sent up a silent prayer that she wouldn't make a complete buffoon of things—again.

Once in the air, Megan reclined her seat, ready to relax.

"Here's the tentative schedule for the week," Jordan read from his laptop.

Megan snapped to attention, flipped her seat back in place, rubbed her tired eyes, and dug in her shoulder bag for a note pad.

"Once we check in at the hotel we can relax until evening when we are expected to attend the formal reception."

"What formal reception? How formal?" She stared at his bent head, his eyes focused on the screen. She mentally inventoried her wardrobe as she'd packed it that morning. Did she have something suitable for a formal event?

"You did pack formal attire, right?"

"I don't recall you mentioning a formal event. But yes, I did pack something that should be suitable for just such an occasion."

She'd thrown her classic black dress she'd bought at the Salvation Army a year ago in her suitcase at the last minute. She'd prayed it still fit when she'd wrestled it out from the back of her closet.

"Good. Now, the following morning, the conference will start at 10:00 a.m. and run until 12:00 p.m. After lunch, we head out to check a few of the crops in the upper delta region. We'll meet with the local farmers. I assume you haven't seen the Pyramids, so if you wish, you can hook up with a tour organized for conference attendees on the way back from the fields. They'll make sure everyone gets back to the hotel in time for the evening meal."

Was he kidding? Of course she'd never seen the Pyramids. Well, maybe in the history books, on postcards, calendars, and on the internet when she'd searched for information about Egypt yesterday.

Not missing a beat, Jordan continued.

"I'm scheduled to attend a separate meeting with the Egyptian representatives after the meal. I expect you to accompany me to take notes. Then the day after, part of the team will fly to Aswan to visit farmers in the region along the Nile Delta. We'll go directly to Luxor instead." He scrolled down. The screen changed. "In Luxor, several of us will do an early morning hot air balloon ride along the Nile to observe the farming methods from above. You'll have to be ready rather early."

"Wait, what? Hot air balloon? As in up off the ground in a small basket with nothing but fire shooting flames up into a rubber balloon?" Megan sat on the edge of her seat, her hands clasped tight, her heart rate soared, her head buzzed. *Should she put her head between her knees? What a nightmare!*

"Yes, perfectly safe. Nothing to worry about." He lifted his head, regarded her, shook his head, and concentrated on his laptop once again. "You'll be fine. I'm sure you brought plenty of Dramamine with you. Now, you'll have to take notes on the various techniques as we drift over the numerous fields to document methods in progress. Following, there will be a brief luncheon meeting, but we'll have the afternoon free. If you want, I can arrange a couple of tours if you are interested. Perhaps one to the Valley of the Kings?"

More tours? This was beginning to sound more like a pleasure trip than an assignment. If she'd known she was going to be doing so much sightseeing she would have asked her friend Lindsey for a few pointers on tourism. She would have done a bit more research on something other than farming practices in the region. She most definitely would have planned accordingly.

"Whatever you suggest will be fine."

"Let's see how much time we'll have after the conference. We'll have another full day of field visits before we fly back to Cairo. There are several more field visits in the northern region of Egypt, then final conference meetings, which should take up another two to three days."

"Thanks for the itinerary, but I was hoping you would fill me in on what is expected of me, what the project involves, and what results are anticipated."

"I was just about to get to that." He shifted a few papers on his lap and hit a few keys on his laptop. "Okay. The watered down version—Wild and Wonderful has teamed up with the University to promote a program we hope will be accepted by the Egyptian Ministry of Agriculture. There are a couple other universities at the conference vying for the contract. Working for a sustainable agriculture tenet, we're confident our methods are geared toward the various Egyptian climates and will enable the growers to enhance the production of their crops, be it wheat, cotton, or any number of their fruits and vegetables, to insure production will be able to feed the growing population."

"Who else is vying for this position?"

"We'll find out when we get there, but we do know at least one organization from Germany and England. Word is there will be agricultural professionals from around the globe giving talks."

"And I fit in with this project, how?"

"As a representative from Wild and Wonderful, you insure we adhere to the principles of good land stewardship, as usual. We'll take the required soil and water samples to help us decide the best method to help them with sustainability. Keep your ears and eyes open. Two heads are better than one, and with your position at Wild and Wonderful, we want to make sure we don't damage any 'sacred' ground or possible sites that might contain antiquities. We might not be aware of these sites, but there are those who don't care and will be careless. We need to pay attention to the talks, look for signs that might be helpful to our research. Take notes. Inform me immediately if you notice anything that doesn't seem right."

Was he asking her to play a spy? Good Lord! A spy! She couldn't keep a secret if her life depended on it. Take notes, maybe, but spy? She must have misunderstood. If it weren't for her needing this job and a good recommendation, she'd tell him just what she thought of his plan and turn around and catch the next flight back home. She didn't even know what she was supposed to look for among a conference full of international professionals. The only language she could speak other than English, was French, and then it had been forever since she'd had to use it. Too bad Helen didn't need her in France.

"What exactly do you want me to look for?"

"I'm sure you'll pick up on it when you hear or see it. As for the basic information being conducted during the conference, you'll recognize the subject matter seeing as you took my class a few years ago. As I recall, you passed it with flying colors."

It hadn't been a particularly great time to have been in his class, what with the crackdown on the sexual student/teacher relationships that had been reported. She hoped he didn't think she had been involved in any of the shenanigans that had taken place. One of the girls in her dorm had been involved, which made it look as if she'd also been one of the instigators. Whitney Nash, guilty as sin, had finally admitted she had worked alone, and confessed to having lied about the whole affair. Megan and the other girls in her dorm had breathed a sigh of relief when all was said and done. It didn't help that Jordan Kaine remembered her, which only dredged up unpleasant memories.

She ignored his reference.

"I understand you also took Professor Sampson's class on Crop Production and Management."

How did he know? Had he checked up on her? Read her transcript?

"Yes, as a matter of fact, I did. Along with a couple of other natural resource classes," she confirmed.

"I know. Which makes you better qualified for this trip than Darla. By the way, Sampson will meet us at the conference. He's on our joint committee."

Before she could respond, the attendant entered, served Hors d'oeuvres and drinks, and then took orders for their evening meal. As much as Megan would love something strong to drink right about now, she knew better than to ask for alcohol while taking Dramamine.

Instead, she ordered a ginger ale, hoping it would help ease the butterflies currently doing a dance in her stomach despite the motion sickness tablet she'd taken back in New York. Being this close to Jordan Kaine elicited memories better left buried in the sand. It hadn't helped that Lindsey had put such fantasy thoughts in her mind.

Chapter Four

Lack of sleep, the long overnight flight, and the time change left what little energy Megan had, dead and gone. Watching Jordan sleep like a baby during the flight, eat as if it was his last meal, and get off the flight with a jaunty lift to his step made her foul mood even worse. Now that they were on solid ground, hopefully once she got some sleep, and the Dramamine was out of her system, she would be herself again. And coffee! Strong coffee laced with extra sugar and cream. She prayed the hotel where they were staying had plenty on hand.

True to Jordan's detailed agenda, they were whisked through the airport, luggage claimed, customs, visas stamped in their passports, and directed to a waiting taxi. He had better organizational skills than she did, and she was no slouch.

The ride from the airport to the hotel was nothing, if not eye-opening. Tall, modern buildings lined either side of the Nile River. A wide promenade extended for blocks at the water's edge with benches located at strategic intervals where one could sit and observe the activity along the river. Small feluccas—Egyptian style sailboats, their white sails puffed out in the breeze reminded her of miniature pirate ships as they gently glided past larger barges. Dock-side, riverboats were loading tourists. Another boat sailed by in the opposite direction. Several young couples sat cuddled arm in arm, wide smiles evident that they were enjoying a romantic interlude. Romantic fantasies filled Megan's thoughts—oh, to sail along on one of those ancient-looking feluccas while held in the arms of someone you loved. Her heart fluttered, her skin warmed as she sat next to Jordan in the taxi. Thoughts of Jordan Kaine came to mind as being the one to satisfy those, and other fantasies, thanks to Lindsey's suggestions. No way was she about to act on them. There was too much at stake, and she didn't need another rejection like Rick's once Jordan discovered she was responsible for her mother's care.

The taxi turned and crossed the *Qasr al-Nil* bridge over the wide expanse of the Nile. Within minutes they were winding up over the highway and looking down on *Tahrir* Square where all the protesters had rioted in 2011. Today it looked peaceful with the American University of Cairo, Egyptian government buildings, the Cairo Museum of Egyptian Antiquities within walking distance, and people going about their business. Now that she was in Egypt and had time to reflect, she wished she did have ample time to explore the museums and temples, and all the other important historic sites. However, she had a job to do and needed to keep focused on helping to secure the Egyptian contract on sustainable horticulture production practices and water management along the Nile to improve crop production. She had to remember she wasn't a tourist, and this wasn't a vacation.

After they arrived at the large modern hotel, Jordan helped her from the cab. Their driver removed their luggage from the trunk and placed them on the cart that had magically appeared curb-side. Jordan took care of the tip, and then together they followed the porter into the opulent reception area. A hotel steward met them at the glass sliding doors glistening in the afternoon sun and escorted them to the front desk. Megan's head buzzed from lack of sleep and the surreal opulent surroundings of the hotel's interior. Plush carpet, crystal chandeliers, glass walls overlooking the city, and colorful floral arrangements were everywhere.

Registration took seconds before they were directed to the panel of elevators with a promise that their luggage would be delivered shortly to their suite.

"Are our rooms next to each other?" Megan didn't want to be too far away from Jordan in case she needed help with something. Being alone in a foreign land for the first time had her biting the inside of her cheek, wanting to turn tail and run back home.

"Actually, we're sharing a suite. It's more economical and convenient. And Greg Sampson will be next door."

"Oh. Okay." So much for her thinking she could keep her distance from Jordan Kaine, especially after the conference meetings were over for the evening. There would be no escaping him. No privacy. This did not bode well for her sanity, and the musings she'd been conjuring—again thanks to Lindsey. She'd already had a hard time keeping her heartbeats under control sitting so close to him in the aircraft, and the tight fit in the taxi ride from the airport—legs and arms were forced tightly against each other. His scent—she was still trying to figure out the spices in his enticing and sexy cologne—musk for sure, but something more that seemed to linger. It had her insides squirming as it surrounded her like a seductive cloak. And now! Holy cow! She had to share a suite with him. She could only hope the bedrooms were on opposite ends of the suite.

On the other hand, at least now she wouldn't have to worry about being alone in a foreign country on her own. He'd be close at hand if she needed him.

Think positive, Meg. You can get through this.

One day at a time.

Her chest rose as she took in a deep, fortifying breath. She clutched her shoulder purse, took another deep breath, and shrugged her shoulders back.

Jordan opened the door and motioned for her to enter ahead of him. He switched the light on, closed the door, and set his carry tote on a chair. Megan stood in the middle of the opulent room, did a 360 degree turn, and made the mistake of focusing on Jordan's seductive eyes.

"Umm…, er…, are you sure this is our room?"

"Of course. You don't like it?"

"What's not to like? It's perfect."

The sitting room alone was made for romance, seduction, and a lover's tryst all rolled into one. She changed her mind. She'd rather have a single room all to herself. Her feelings for Jordan were going to be hard to keep under wraps if she had to stay with him in this incredible suite for very long. The muted tones, the artistic paintings of ancient antiquities—why it had to be Queen Nefertiti and King Tut in matching frames over the small, but elegant fireplace trimmed in white marble. And the brass statues scattered around the room. An elegant black and gold Egyptian-style serving tray sat in the middle of the mahogany coffee table piled high with fresh fruit. The lamp shades on the end tables either side of the sofa represented the pale pink lotus blossom fanned out in full bloom. A matching fragrance filled the room.

Definitely a room made for seduction. She wasn't sure she wanted to see the bedroom. At least there were two of them.

"I hadn't expected such grand, romantic accommodations."

"Not to worry, you're safe—you have nothing to fear from me. My mind is focused on gaining this contract."

Well, that put her in her place. He had no feelings for her, which was going to make working with him much easier. Maybe. Now all she had to do was get some sleep and get her mind focused back on the tasks at hand—mainly making it through the conference with flying colors and securing her job with Wild and Wonderful.

"Are you sure you don't want Professor Sampson to share this suite with you? The two of you probably have more to discuss then the two of us."

"He requested a single."

Perhaps she should have, as well, instead of assuming she'd have her own accommodations.

She crossed to the balcony's glass sliding door and drew the sheer curtains aside. A wicker table and four chairs to the right of the balcony provided plenty of room for entertaining outside overlooking Cairo and the Nile. Megan looked out over the city—the sun gleamed off the Nile, the tall buildings on either side of the river confirmed Cairo's importance in the 21st Century. She was both uneasy and excited to explore the City of a

Thousand Minarets, and the largest metropolitan area in the Middle East.

"You can choose which room you'd like. I was assured they each had their own bath facilities."

"It really doesn't matter to me."

"Okay, then. Why don't you take the room on the left and I'll take the one on the right?"

"Sounds good."

They turned to their respective rooms, opening the doors simultaneously. Megan walked into a room fit for a King's harem. If she thought the main room was seduction in a nutshell, this bedroom was sexual anticipation. Red, gold, and black bedspread and pillow cases. Thick brocade draperies covered the canopied bed. Plush matching carpet so deep her feet sank to her ankles. An Egyptian motif boarder circled the mirrored ceiling that cried take me. She wasn't sure she wanted to check out the accommodating facilities.

Oh! My! God! Sinful was the only word to describe the huge walk in shower, done entirely in ceramic hieroglyphic tiles she was sure had some kind of sexual inference. Was Jordan's room and facilities as impressive? As intimidating? As sexual?

Heat radiated from her toes to the top of her head, the hairs on her neck prickled. No way could she stay in this room for an entire week and not think about Jordan Kaine sleeping—alone—in a bed mere yards from her own.

She might just as well accept defeat and return home and look for another job.

Still, she wanted to kick off her shoes, lie down, curl up, close her eyes, and wish the world away. But she couldn't. There was no time. She had to prepare for the evening reception. And save her job to make sure her mother had essential health care. She should call Lindsey. Tell her she had arrived safely, and check in on her mother's condition.

****

Jordan's heart stuttered the second he walked into his room. Bringing Megan Holloway to Egypt with him was a colossal mistake. Just looking at the huge king-size canopy bed, draped in heavy gold-gilded fabric and matching cord strings had his lower extremities standing at attention. Envisioning Megan lying on that bed naked—next to him…

Stop it. It is not gonna happen.

He had a job to do, and he was damn well going to do it.

Concentrate, Kaine. Seal the bid for the contract. Get your head out of your ass and do your job. You don't need another sexual harassment situation to screw up your tenure.

Jordan tossed his laptop on the silk covered feather-tic coverlet, made his way to the john and did a double take. *Holy hell!* The open shower stall with the many shower nozzles jutting out from all three walls had his mind buzzing with possibilities that seeing the bed hadn't managed to conjure up yet. A groan escaped as he swiveled around on his deck shoes and headed out of the bedroom.

And came face to face with the woman who had just taken center stage in his recent shower fantasy.

"I hope your accommodations are to your liking." His certainly were to his—and more.

The bright rose color covering her cheeks confirmed his suspicions that her room was a duplicate of his. How was he going to last a week, let alone a night, with her sleeping in the other room? Maybe he should have insisted Greg Sampson share the suite with him. He didn't care that Helen was concerned for Megan's safety in a foreign country. His cousin certainly hadn't considered his reputation and the fact that he was up for tenure.

"Yes. Like I said earlier, I'm surprised we were assigned such an opulent suite."

"I suspect all the suites are the same. In reality, Helen said it was best for the budget, rather than paying for two separate rooms."

She looked around the room like a star-struck teenager. A good reminder that she was off limits. Standing there, her emerald eyes sparkled, her lower lip pulled in by her teeth with her upper lip pressed over top—hell, he wanted to kiss her worries away. Ahh, damn. Her chest—her enticing breasts—rose and fell with every deep breath she took. Good God. He had to get out of this suite. Now!

"Let's go register for the conference, beat the crowd. Check out the hotel so we know where everything is, where the meeting rooms, restaurant, and bar are located. I spotted a marquee in the lobby when we came in. It probably contains information about the conference."

"Good idea. I've never been in such a huge and magnificent hotel before. I don't want to get lost on the first day. Give me a minute to freshen up."

"You look fine."

"Really. I need a minute."

So did he.

Jordan sank into the plush sofa, the minute she left the room. He snatched a couple of ripe purple grapes from the fruit assortment on the coffee table, popped them in his mouth, shut his eyes, and leaned his head against the velvety material. He needed to focus on the project rather than on the sexy Megan Holloway.

It was going to be a long, tortuous week.

****

The reception area was abuzz with attendees arriving and registering. Megan sat on one of the assorted chairs arranged in a social setting and browsed through the material the conference personnel had handed her. Jordan sat next to her scanning the conference attendees.

"Ah, I see Greg made it." Jordan rose. "If you'll excuse me, I'll go let him know we've registered."

The two men shook hands, and in conversation, ambled back to Megan. She recognized Dr. Sampson right away. His dark wavy hair was a bit too long around the edges and blended with his large bushy eyebrows. He had a slight paunch, suggesting he hadn't seen a gym in ages. Shorter than Jordan, he was at least ten years older. But the professor had always been very polite and helpful in class. If she remembered correctly, his wife was a psychology professor at one of the other local colleges.

"We've already checked into our rooms," Jordan was saying as they approached. "Thought we'd get registered, see who's here so far. Greg, you remember Megan Holloway? Our counterpart from Wild and Wonderful who is working with us. Megan, Gregory Sampson."

"Yes, Miss Holloway. Good to see you on the project. As I recall, you aced my class."

"Professor Sampson." Megan stood and accepted the professor's hand.

"Please, it's Greg, seeing as we're going to be working together. Good to have you on board."

"If you have some time right now we can get a drink and discuss our plan of attack," Jordan suggested. "Go over the final agenda before tonight's event."

"I'm agreeable. Shall we go for a coffee?" Greg stepped aside, switched his registration packet to his left hand, and waited for Megan and Jordan to precede him.

"Coffee sounds wonderful." Megan needed the caffeine, due to the time change, if she was going to stay awake in order to get through the rest of the day and the reception later tonight. She stepped to the side and followed the men, who were once again in deep conversation. Her head still throbbed from the long flight and lack of sleep. If it weren't for needing to know what their plans were and wanting to do everything she could in order to get a good review, she'd go back to her room and take a nap.

The restaurant server greeted them, then ushered them to a small, secluded table next to a window overlooking an expansive courtyard, and the bridge spanning *Tahrir* Square. The sun was high in the sky and sparkled through the large windowpane. A rectangular panel along the top did little to deflect the glare. Megan slid into the padded chair, her back to the window, the men settled on either side of the table.

A waitress hurried to their table and took their order for coffee and a confection.

"I've already talked to the Assistant to the Chair of Cairo's Agricultural Ministry earlier." Greg folded his hands on top of his placemat. "He seems interested in our proposal for a more sustainable production module. It fits in with Egypt's mission and objectives to achieve sustainable development though the implementation of modern technology. I'm sure others will be cognizant of their mission, too. So we'll have to be vigilant to what others are suggesting."

"Of course." Jordan leaned forward. "Like you said, your presentation should go a long way to convince them we are in a position to join their international team. Our university is number one in the field of horticulture. That alone should prove to them we are the best team to help with their research, extension, and training programs."

"So how does Wild and Wonderful fit into this program?" The two men looked at her, eyebrows raised as if they'd just remembered she was present. "I understand the company's mission is to make sure various programs and projects don't disrupt indigenous people and endanger flora and fauna, but how does that relate to this international joint project with the university?" She needed more information than what Jordan had shared on the plane.

"Just that," Jordan said.

His lips turned up at the corners, his dimples smiling as he studied her with a focus that had her insides humming. The sun made his eyes shimmer—the pupils wide and consuming. Day one and she was already affected by his smoky gray eyes that left her mesmerized.

Oh, Lord, what had she just asked him? Oh, yes…, something about how Wild and Wonderful fit into the scheme of things. She had to get her mind back on the project.

"Our team wants the project. We feel we are a good fit for what they want to accomplish—that of providing more and better produce for their growing population," Jordan said, bringing her back to the current conversation. "It would be an enormous feather in our cap. We also want to make sure the Egyptian government and the Agricultural Ministry know we are serious about making sure we implement it ecologically and in a respectful manner."

The waitress delivered their strong aromatic coffee and placed a delicate fluted dish next to their cups filled with a thick slice of pound cake covered with fresh raspberries, blueberries, and strawberries. Megan breathed in the fruity essence as she thanked the young woman. She attacked her coffee, enjoying the hot brew full of caffeine, and then dug into the sinful looking dessert. The men did likewise before continuing their dialogue.

"Farmers are always uncovering some form of antiquity." Greg set his cup back in the saucer and folded his arms on the edge of the table. "We need to make sure we don't inadvertently destroy such sites or important finds. We need to be cognizant of the local's beliefs and way of life while we collect samples of the soil and of various crops."

"Thus, we have Wild and Wonderful on board." Jordan held his fork in his left hand ready to slice into his cake. "Wild and Wonderful has had a big presence and impact in other countries around the world, as you are aware, Greg. Their track record is stellar. Helen jumped at the chance to be included in this project. In fact, she wanted to be the one to join the team, but she's tied up in France for the foreseeable future."

"And my part in this?" Megan asked. "Other than to keep my eyes and ears open as you suggested, I presume, is to make sure these objectives are met?"

"Exactly." Jordan popped a heaping forkful of cake and berries into his mouth, lifted his coffee with his right hand, and took a long draw of the hot brew.

"At least now I have a better idea of what I'm doing here. What I'm looking and listening for among the other attendees." She held her cup to her lips, ready to indulge, but held out waiting for Jordan's reply.

Greg's head darted back and forth between the two of them as if he were at a tennis match. Megan had the urge to giggle at the amused look on his face, but she was too upset with Jordan for holding this bit of information back while he had filled her in on their agenda on the plane.

"I had a lot on my mind at the time. I thought it wise to wait to include Greg in the conversation. I was right. I suggest we finish our coffee and head back to our rooms to rest before we get ready for the reception later this evening." He turned to Greg. "Unless you have something more to add to the conversation, I'll see you at the opening conference at 4:30." He raised his brows.

"Me? No. That about sums it up for now. By the way, are you planning to meet with your father and brother at their latest dig?"

"Yes, I'm hoping to find time to meet with them when we visit the Nile Delta in the Luxor Valley."

So Jordan's father was an archeologist. It must be exciting digging up history. Especially here in Egypt, where they were continuingly uncovering the past—the cradle of civilization.

"I think I'll go for a stroll along the river," Greg interrupted her thoughts. "Stretch my legs a bit after our long flight. Care to join me?"

"Thanks, I'd rather go over my notes one more time before things get under way." Jordan pushed his chair back and rose at the same time, ready to leave. "I'll catch up with you later tonight."

"What about you, Megan?" Greg invited. "Care to check out the Nile?"

About to refuse, she changed her mind, not wanting to be cooped up in the suite with Jordan for the rest of the afternoon.

"I'd love to. Give me a minute to use the facilities and I'll meet you in the foyer."

Chapter Five

Megan was thankful Jordan wasn't waiting for her when she returned from the walk along the Nile with Professor Sampson. She went to her room to prepare for the evening event. Greg had filled her in on Jordan's father and brother's escapades as Egyptologists and archeologists. She was intrigued to learn that Jordan's father, Henry Kaine, had connections with Cairo University, and was in Egypt working on the latest discovery. He had also participated on the research on King Tut's tomb in the Valley of the Kings. She just might take Jordan up on the invitation to tour the Valley of the Kings if time permitted when they visited Luxor.

Megan lifted the hanger from the narrow closet, removed her basic black dress, and laid it on the bed. She hadn't had a chance to try it on before she left New York and became conscious of her mistake the minute she slipped it on over her head and adjusted the straps. She stood in front of the floor-length mirror attached to the back of the closet door and gaped at her image. The low-cut neckline and scalloped edges above her breasts emphasized their fullness. The thin spaghetti straps exposed her shoulders and highlighted her bare neck.

Naked! OMG! She was naked.

She should never have let Lindsey talk her into shopping at Victoria's Secret. Her barely-there uplifting strapless bra and silky undies did little to bolster her confidence. She didn't care what her friend said. If it wasn't for the tight bodice holding the empire waist dress in place, those loose straps would be down around her ankles, along with the dress that whispered sensually just below the knees. She'd decided to stick with a low sling-back black pump, as she hadn't worn heels in months, not having any special events to attend since her breakup with Rick.

Letting Lindsey talk her into cutting her hair so short, was another huge mistake. It might be easier to take care of while traveling, but it left her feeling much more vulnerable. At least with longer hair it would have covered her neck and shoulders. She wouldn't feel as if she was on display.

She slipped into her pumps, grabbed her shoulder purse, and sucked in a deep breath. Ready or not, she had to make it through the night. Too much depended on it.

She stepped from her room and paused. Jordan stood next to the balcony door facing the city lights sparkling in the background. His hands were clasped behind his back as if he was contemplating the fate of the world. His formal dark gray suit fit his trim body to perfection—not a single crease or spare inch of material could be seen from this angle. He turned. His smoky-gray eyes shot wide when he spotted her.

"You look lovely tonight." He took a tentative step forward, and then stopped. "I see you found something suitable to wear. I dare say, Megan Holloway, you might just give everyone pause when they see you in that dress tonight. Certainly going to give the other women a run for their money."

"I'm not trying to compete with anyone. Perhaps I should change."

"Don't bother on my account. However, you might want to grab a wrap. The culture here is a bit different than ours back home when it comes to women's modesty."

Blood rushed up her neck, and warmth washed over her cheeks. Why hadn't Lindsey said something? Instead of taking her to Victoria's Secret, she should have gone to the local discount store.

"Ummm…, I'll go find something more suitable to wear." She hesitated. What could she wear? She had only packed the one dress.

"Do you have another dress?"

Had he read her mind so easily?

"You said to pack light. You should have been more specific."

"A scarf perhaps?"

"Umm…"

"No problem. We can stop at one of the boutique shops in the hotel on our way to the reception."

"I'm sorry, I don't have extra money. I'm on a tight budget as it is."

"My treat. Are you ready?"

"Oh, no. I don't expect you to buy me one."

"It's no problem."

"I'll reimburse you when we return to New York."

"Not necessary. Think of it as a souvenir from Egypt."

Megan vowed to repay him. Taking gifts from Jordan Kaine, no matter how formally given out of necessity on a business trip, somehow didn't seem right. She didn't want him to think she was one of those women who expected a man to pay her way. And she wasn't about to expend any more of Wild and Wonderful's advance on such items.

Chills ran from her shoulders to her fingertips, from her spine all the way to her toes despite the warmth that crept up through the tips of the roots of her hair. If Jordan didn't stop looking at her with those sexy eyes of his, as if she was standing there naked, she was going to run back to her room and lock the door. And never come out.

"Well, shall we go then?" He stepped past her to open the door.

She could only follow, and hope the evening wasn't the disaster it was starting out to be.

The boutique was in a separate corridor along with several other small up-scale shops. A heavy scent of citrus incense filled the small interior as they entered. Jordan led her toward a tiny enclave displaying many silk scarves in varying colorful shades and designs. A young salesgirl came to their aid. Dressed in a more modern Egyptian-styled *tob sebleh*—the dress wasn't as flowing or as long as the ones she'd seen other women on the streets wear. The salesgirl wore snug trousers underneath her dress, instead of the baggy *tshalvar*.

"May I help, madam?" Her voice held a light accent, easily understood.

"The lady would like to purchase a scarf to go with her dress." Jordan's smile caught the young girl's attention.

"Ah, I have the perfect one. Come."

She led them to a row of scarves hanging on a series of pegs along the side wall. She ran her hand along the wraps. The scarves fluttered as if a wind had whooshed through the selection. The sales girl stopped at an emerald green silk wrap with knotted tassels on either end, and lifted it off its peg. The material fluttered over the women's shoulder and arm as she extended her hand and displayed the scarf for Jordan's inspection.

"Perfect," Jordan whispered.

Megan raised her eyes at the obvious 'male dominant' exchange.

"It matches your eyes and highlights the ginger tones in your hair. We'll take it," he addressed the sales lady before Megan had a chance to respond.

Megan spotted the price tag before the sales lady headed to the cash register behind the counter, scarf in hand. "It's too expensive. I can't afford it."

Jordan's eyebrows rose. His mouth tightened. He shook his head, then opened his wallet and drew out a few Egyptian Pounds and handed them over the counter. "We'll discuss it later. Right now, we don't want to be late."

Jordan wrapped the scarf around her shoulders, his fingertips brushing against her exposed skin. His touch was warm, barely there, like the flutter of butterfly wings. She averted her eyes, afraid he would see in them how his touch affected her insides. Instead, she looked up and caught the sales lady's full, blood red lips rise, ever so slightly in an all-knowing smile, as if she'd just witnessed a lovers' touching exchange. To make matters worse, Jordan put his arm around her waist and ushered her out the door. The temperature surrounding her rose by degrees, and it had nothing to do with the new wrap that covered her like a cocoon. At least now she didn't feel so naked. Although with

Jordan's body warmth, his heady cologne, and his touch that elicited erotic thoughts, she might just as well be naked.

****

A modern, local band located in the far corner of the patio played a mixture of Western, Asian, and Egyptian numbers. The humid evening air and exotic scents drifting in around the open-air terrace were unexpectedly stimulating. Scents from the breeze coming off the Nile mixed with the various blooms surrounding them, and no doubt the fragrance of the spices used in the many hors d'oeuvres waitresses were in the process of serving heightened Megan's senses. She hoped a visit to a spice market was on their agenda.

A manicured flowering Paris-style garden surrounded the edges of the wide tiled floor. Plush tropical palm trees shaded the terrace, forming a private border on the far side of the enclosure. Rattan chairs draped with pink damask material, tied with wide white ribbons in the back were strategically placed next to large white tables, also covered with white damask tablecloths—lanterns glowed in the center of each table.

Had she stepped into a fairytale? All she needed now was her prince charming to arrive and carry her off on his galloping white steed. Okay, so she was getting her fairytales mixed up. Being raised on Cinderella had made her a wee-bit partial to that happily-ever-after. But Aladdin was more like it. She sighed. Someone touched her arm. Jordan. Her heart thumped erratically, bringing her out of her silly childhood fantasies. She blinked, looked at him, only to find that he was directing his attention to two men who were approaching, smiles on their faces. The taller of the two reminded her of Omar Sharif in Lawrence of Arabia.

"You finally made it, I see." Greg smiled, and then turned to the man on his left. "Jordan, you remember Mr. Salah Delagad from the University of Cairo. Mr. Delagad, this is Megan Holloway from the Wild and Wonderful Corporation in New York. She's working with us on our proposed project I mentioned."

"Yes, I remember Salah," Jordan said. He extended his hand in greeting. "How have you been, my friend?"

"Good. Good. Happy to meet you again, Jordan. And Miss Holloway." Selah Delagad stepped forward, enveloped her hand in his and nodded. "Charmed to meet you."

"It's nice to meet you, too, Mr. Delagad."

"It is my pleasure to introduce you to a few of the others that you most surely should meet. Come, we will partake of some of the refreshments first, and then we will circulate."

Megan joined the men, drinks in hand, as Mr. Delagad introduced them to many of the members of the Egyptian team. Try as she might, it was hard to keep up with the Egyptian names, although a couple of the men stood out as very friendly, open, and appreciative that the American's were there to assist in their endeavor to find ways in which to feed their growing population. She attempted to gauge Jordan and Greg's impression of the men, whose poker faces gave nothing away.

"If you'll excuse me, I see another friend of my father's," Jordan said as he turned to Megan. "I'd like to have a word with him. Stick by Greg. He'll see you're introduced to anyone else we need to connect with tonight."

"Of course." Greg extended his elbow toward Megan. "Let's go have a word with the team from Norway. I see Mr. Stephenssen, an old acquaintance."

Megan accepted Greg's arm as Jordan disappeared through the crowd. Overwhelmed by the large international gathering, she was relieved not to have been left on her own.

****

Jordan crossed the paved patio to join his father's friend—one of the Egyptologists who worked with his father on several of their digs.

"Dr. Nagid. How have you been? Unearthed any special artifacts lately?"

"Professor Kaine. What a pleasant surprise to see you at the conference. Have you talked to your father yet?" Omar Nagid extended his hand in greeting.

"I am hoping to catch up with him when we go to Luxor. I'm surprised you aren't supervising the operation."

"Yes, although I have been a bit distracted with other projects at the moment. So much activity with the new boat that has been uncovered, and now another burial site near the Valley of the Kings. Have you heard of it?"

"My father mentioned it the last time we talked, but I've been occupied getting our proposal together for the conference. What are you doing here? Are you giving a talk?"

"Yes, yes. As you know many digs are the outcome of farmers discovering such finds. So, it is my wish to be sure that those who are involved in agricultural projects are made aware of the possibility of such occurrences."

"Then you will be glad to know our university team has enlisted the help of the Wild and Wonderful Corporation to make sure that just such a possibility doesn't happen. In fact, Miss Megan Holloway is here with me. I will be happy to introduce you. I'm sure the two of you will have much to discuss."

"It will be my honor to share my views with her. Perhaps we can meet tomorrow before the conference gets underway. I would suggest tonight; however, I am already due elsewhere in a few moments."

"We'll see you tomorrow morning, then."

"I look forward to it, my friend."

Jordan shook hands with Dr. Nagid in farewell. About to join Megan and Greg, he turned and bumped into the woman he hoped never to see again. He recognized her cloying perfume, her sexy come-hither look, and whiny voice. Shit! Whitney Nash!

"Well, well, Professor Kaine. I had no idea you'd be here. Although I'm not surprised your university is vying for this contract, as well."

Of all people. Who would have the balls to hire her, let alone trust her to represent their company for such an important position? Apparently, they either hadn't checked her college records carefully enough, or she'd changed her ways. Or she'd used her sexual charms to get what she wanted. In any case, he needed to be cautious where she was concerned.

"Hello, Miss Nash. Yes, we've teamed up with a grassroots organization to promote sustainability."

He would not mention their past involvement, such as it was, because it wasn't anything he wanted to dredge up. Ever again. Seeing her here after all these years only prompted memories of the nightmare she'd put him through. He'd be wise to keep an eye on her. Was Megan aware that Whitney was here? As he recalled, they had both been in the same class—his class—the same semester. He was sure Megan had been aware of the situation. Did she hold him responsible? Was that why she seemed reticent to accompany him to Egypt?

Keep it professional, Kaine. Play it cool.

"I'm so glad we've met again. I can only apologize for the awful, immature mess I caused you. I do hope you've been able to forgive me."

And there it was! Was her apology sincere? Her lowered voice, her eyes darting around the room as if making sure no one was within hearing range, her wringing hands—was it a sign of her true regret? A nervousness, a lack of confidence so unlike the younger girl he knew years ago? The student who had made his life a living hell with her unfounded sexual harassment charges?

"It's in the past where it belongs, Miss Nash." He could only hope her mentioning it now wasn't going to come back to bit him on the butt—again.

"I'm so glad you feel that way, too. I wouldn't want to let it interfere with our professional relationship here at the conference. I really looked up to you as a professor. I hear you're up for tenure."

How the hell did she know he was up for tenure? And was that a tat on her left shoulder peeking out from between long strands of her wheat-blonde hair?

"Yes, well, it's in the works. What company did you say you're representing?"

"I'm the Assistant Marketing Director with Sutton Ag Solutions out of California. I finished my degree out there. I'm giving a talk on Modern Agriculture Technology. What about you? Something to do with sustainability, no doubt."

"Yes, Sustainable Agriculture for the Growing Population."

"I can't wait to hear it, although after taking your class, it would prove to be a refresher course, I'm sure. We should meet for coffee—catch up."

Was she kidding? The last thing he wanted was to 'catch up' with Whitney Nash. Alone!

"I'll have to double check our team's schedule. It's already filling up."

"I'm sure you can find a smidgen of time somewhere in your busy schedule." She rested her hand on his sleeve, her smile evocative. "Besides, we'll be traveling to many of the same sites together."

"Of course. I'm sure my team would be able to join you. You might remember Professor Sampson, and Megan Holloway."

"Megan Holloway?" The startled look on her face was priceless. Her wide eyes at the news lowered as a coy smile spread across her suddenly pale face. "Megan's here? Don't tell me she works at the university now?"

"No. She's employed with the Wild and Wonderful Corporation. We're working on the Egyptian project together, like I mentioned. In fact, if you'll excuse me, I should be getting back to my team."

"Great. I'll accompany you. It'll be good to see Megan again."

****

"I assume you are aware Habib El-Said has given instructions to put a tail on Jordan Kaine and his entourage during their stay in Egypt." Salah Delagad stood with his back against the side of the hotel, out of sight behind the trash receptacle and the large metal air conditioner—the constant hum muffled their voices.

"So, you have spoken with Habib?" Omar Nagid said, leaning close to Salah. "Yes, I am aware. I have had much contact with Henry Kaine and his work on site, as you know, and as part of the university, and thus the conference. I will have no problem staying close to Jordan Kaine and his people, as well."

"Do not do anything rash," Salah warned. "Only to keep an eye on things and report to me if you suspect anything that might compromise the 'dig.' Jordan Kaine will no doubt visit his father at the current site. And they have a representative from Wild and Wonderful, an American company that is on hand to make sure the university they represent is on the up and up. Perhaps you should keep a close eye on Megan Holloway, get her on our side," Salah said.

"I have met her already. But there is another American woman—a Whitney Nash." Omar's eyebrows rose over squinty eyes, his smile a sneer. "She is a very beautiful woman and appears to be very attracted to Jordan Kaine. What is their connection? Perhaps we should keep an eye on her, as well."

"I'd prefer you watch the Holloway woman," Salah said. "I suspected a stronger connection between her and Jordan Kaine—perhaps a better link to the artifacts through his father."

"Who is watching Henry Kaine?" Omar asked.

"Ah, that would be Habib himself." Salah Delagad sighed. "He is housed over the hill in the sand hut. I will meet with him when the conference attendees fly to Luxor. In the meantime, you need to report any findings to me and I will report to Habib."

Salah wanted to be kept in the loop. If things got out of control, he was going to back out—artifacts or no artifacts. No matter who claimed them or walked off with them. Rumor had it that the Green Dragons of New York had started up again. It had been several years since they had been shut down after the Shanghai incident. If Habib was involved with smuggling, Salah was going to have to keep a close eye on the man's schemes.

****

"Is that who I think it is standing next to Jordan?" Greg's brows shot up. Drink in hand, he pointed in the couple's direction. "What the hell is she doing here? Good Lord, this doesn't bode well. I wonder whose program she represents?"

Megan gulped the remainder of her ginger ale, blinked in disbelief, and couldn't take her eyes off Whitney Nash. Still a sexy bombshell, she was wrapped around Jordan like a long-lost lover. And Jordan appeared to be lapping it up—again! She had to agree with Greg—this didn't bode well at all.

"I haven't seen her since…" she paused, catching herself just in time, not wanting to be the one to mention Jordan's past. She'd heard the rumors but didn't know the entire story. Perhaps there had been some truth to it after all.

"Yes. The 'incident'," Greg groaned. "From the looks of the two of them, I don't think Jordan learned his lesson. How well did you know her, and what she did to Jordan?"

"She was in my class and lived in my dorm. We were never really what you would call close friends—she ran with a different crowd."

"I'm glad to hear it. I hope she doesn't cause any trouble while we're here. I'd hate to lose this contract. I don't trust her one inch."

Megan didn't either. Seeing Whitney Nash cozy up to Jordan had her insides bunching. Whitney's dress covered more skin than her own black dress, but Whitney's blood-red dress looked like it cost a million bucks, was skin tight and accentuated her curvy, well-proportioned sexy body. The black three-inch heels, long blonde hair, expertly applied makeup, and sensuous smile made Megan feel like the country bumpkin who didn't stand a chance in any fairytale of ever attracting a man. So much for her fairytale—not that she considered she had a chance with Jordan. She had enough on her plate with keeping her job and taking care of her mother at the moment.

With balled fists, Megan tugged her scarf around the front of her tired body and sighed. Her mother's health was her main concern. Besides, what man would want to be saddled with someone who was the sole provider for their ill mother? Certainly Rick Simon hadn't. The lowlife had dropped her so fast the minute he assumed she was a package deal. He'd made his point clear—he wasn't about to take on someone else's responsibilities. He hadn't even had the nerve to tell her face to face—he'd called it quits in a text on her cell phone. The coward.

"How Jordan could have let himself be caught up in that woman's clutches in the first place is beyond me," Greg interrupted her thoughts. "And here she is again. I know it's none of my business, but I think we should go rescue him—save him from himself. Or her."

"Really, Greg, I don't want to interfere. Like you said, it's none of my business."

"I don't think we have a choice. Here they come."

Megan wanted to crawl under the table. She wished she had a reason to excuse herself, but nothing came to mind.

"Wow! Megan Holloway. I can't believe it. How wonderful to see you again."

"Whitney. What a surprise. How have you been?" Megan offered her right hand in welcome.

Whitney disengaged her tight grip from around Jordan's arm, and instead of shaking Megan's hand, she wrapped her arms around her—a lightweight, false hug. Her cloying perfume made it difficult for Megan to breathe. The girl hadn't changed at all. Megan glanced at Jordan as he stepped away from Whitney and rubbed the spot on his arm where Whitney had been attached. Poor Jordan.

Whitney acknowledged Professor Sampson in a more professional manner before addressing Megan again.

"I was just telling Jordan we need to meet for coffee—catch up."

"Sounds like a plan." She didn't know about Jordan, but it was the last thing she wanted to do.

"I hear you've landed a great job with a grassroots organization. Right up your alley."

"Yes, well, I haven't been there long, although I've enjoyed the experience so far. It's a reputable company and a great place to work."

"And includes travel. Lucky you to be traveling in such prestigious company as Professor Kaine—and Professor Sampson, of course." Her sexy smile lingered on Jordan before aiming it at Greg. The woman just didn't give up.

Before Megan could reply, the main doors swung open and an entourage of six Egyptians dressed in western black suits, white shirts and ties, along with highly polished shoes, made an impressive entrance, ending the current of conversations scattered around the room.

"The head of the Ministry of Agriculture is in the lead," Whitney whispered as if she had the inside scoop. "I met him earlier today. A very nice gentleman."

Megan could only nod as the crowd hushed and the men made their way to the raised platform to the left of the courtyard. A white canopy with lights overhead, and a string of potted flowering plants lined the stage. Jordan stood next to Greg, while Whitney silently inched forward toward the front of the crowd already gathered in anticipation of the Minister's address.

Megan was relieved at Whitney's abandonment. Forcing herself to push the incident to the back of her mind, she made it a point to listen carefully to the speakers. If she were to do her job well, she needed to have a clear idea of what the ministry wished to achieve at the conference. Greg and Jordan were also engrossed in the men's speeches as they took turns welcoming everyone to Cairo and the conference. A schedule had been prepared ahead of time, and specific time slots were arranged for each of the teams to meet to discuss their project's concepts.

As the evening wound down and others began to depart, Megan spotted Whitney in a far corner under one of the palms talking to Dr. Omar Nagid, one of the speakers Jordan had introduced to her earlier. Having learned he was a friend of Jordan's father, Megan wondered if Whitney was trying to ingratiate herself with the Egyptian in order to further her connection with Jordan. She recalled Greg's concern that Whitney's presence did not bode well.

"We're scheduled to meet with the Egyptian team Monday at four o'clock," Jordan said, as they headed toward the elevator and their rooms later that night. "We'll have plenty of time to assess the situation after we meet with several farmers tomorrow afternoon. Talks will commence after breakfast and run from nine until noon. Buses are scheduled to leave at 1:30."

"When did they say our talk is scheduled?" Greg asked, as he punched the elevator button, then stepped back to wait for the door to slide open.

"Monday afternoon at one o'clock. This will give us plenty of time to make it more pertinent to the local farmers we visit tomorrow, and before the meeting on Monday so we can establish their needs. We're scheduled to leave for Aswan and Luxor in the evening. Our flight leaves at seven o'clock on Monday."

Several other conference attendees crowded into the elevators as soon as the door slid open, making additional conversation impossible. Megan's mind was on overload trying to keep days and times straight and wanting nothing more than to fall into bed and get some sleep. Her mind whirred, contemplating actually being in Egypt, working in close proximity with Jordan, and the fact that Whitney was no doubt going to stir up trouble.

Greg waved goodnight as they exited the elevator. Megan walked alongside Jordan and waited while he inserted the keycard to unlock their shared suite. He stepped aside to let her enter. As it had been a tiring two days traveling without much sleep, she was ready to lie down, shut her eyes, and pray tomorrow would right itself. And that Whitney Nash wasn't going to cause more trouble.

One could only hope.

Chapter Six

"If you'll excuse me, I need to call home to find out how my mother is doing before I call it a night." Megan clutched her evening purse and silk scarf around her shoulders. "Thanks again for the scarf."

"I wasn't aware your mother was ill." Jordan took a step toward her, his brows lowered in concern. "I hope it's nothing serious."

"Unfortunately it was rather severe. She and my step-father were in an auto accident on their way to their Florida home for the winter months. She sustained a broken leg and ankle and had to have surgery. After surgery, she learned Edward had been killed in the crash, and she suffered a stroke. She's in a rehab facility at the moment."

"I'm sorry for your loss. When did this happen?" Jordan asked.

"Thank you. It happened three weeks ago. They hadn't been married long. Still, the shock has delayed the healing process. She's doing as well as can be expected. A close friend of mine is checking in on her while I'm in Egypt."

"Was Helen aware of your situation before she left for France?"

"No. She'd already left before the accident."

"I'm sure she would have made alternative arrangements for someone else to accompany Greg and I, had she known."

Megan was reminded of Darla Slidell. Darla would have jumped at the chance.

"My friend Lindsey is like family. She'll be a comfort to my mother in my absence."

"If there is anything I can do to help, let me know. If you need a sounding board, I'm in the next room."

"Thanks. I'll be fine."

Megan left Jordan standing in the middle of the room. The last thing she needed to do was use Jordan Kaine as a sounding board. She needed to keep their relationship on a professional level.

She changed into her lightweight short night dress Lindsey had insisted she buy—too sheer for her own taste. It was silky, smooth, and soft against her bare skin. She lay on the bed, the cool sheets comforting. She propped the fluffy pillow against the headboard and reached for her cell phone to call Lindsey.

Lindsey answered after the first ring, their friendship and the caller ID number needing no introductions. "Your mother is doing just fine, Megan," Lindsey said as soon as she answered. "Relax and enjoy your time in Cairo."

"Easy for you to say." Megan moved to the edge of the bed and kicked off her slippers. "You're a world traveler. Me? I'm beginning to be spell-bound by Egypt already. Still, I'm hanging on by a thread. I'm sharing a suite with Jordan Kaine. He's in the other bedroom as we speak."

"Lucky you. Aren't you glad I took you to Victoria's Secret to buy all those sexy, slinky undies and nighties?"

"No! And I'm not sure we're going to be friends when I return. I've felt positively naked with this hair cut once I put on my black dress."

"I remember that dress. You rocked it—very sexy. Loved it on you."

"Well, I was a bit underdressed tonight. Jordan bought me a scarf to wrap around my shoulders and cover up my nearly naked chest. I swear, Lindsey, we will have words when I return."

"Sounds like you're off to a great start already—Jordan buying you gifts."

"Get your head out of the gutter." Megan shimmied back into the pillows and crossed her legs. "Jordan Kaine has bigger problems than worrying about getting the Egyptian contract. Whitney Nash showed up. It appears she's working with a company in California and is vying for the same contract."

"Where have I heard her name?"

"She was the one in college who charged Jordan with sexual harassment. Put him and a few others through hell."

"Right. I remember you talking about her. I assumed that was all water under the bridge?"

"I did, too. You should have seen them. The two of them looked all cozy when they met tonight. In fact, she's already ingratiated herself into meeting with us to 'catch up'."

"You need to fight for what you want, girlfriend."

"I need this job, *girlfriend*. I'm not about to do something stupid and lose my job over Jordan Kaine and Whitney Nash. Not my circus."

"Nevertheless, I'm expecting a full report when you return."

"Again. There will be nothing to report. In the meantime, please remember to give me a call if there are any problems with Mom."

"Don't worry. She and her dog are in good hands. You just enjoy the break and give Whitney Nash a run for her money."

"Good night, Lindsey. Give Mom my love. I'll talk to you in a couple of days."

Megan ended the call and slid between the cool sheets, her mind racing in so many directions she was sure she wouldn't get any sleep. Glad to know her mother was doing okay so far, she could focus on tomorrow's schedule.

Jordan hadn't said a word about Whitney Nash and their reunion. She didn't get any vibes from him one way or the other in that regard. Well, like she'd said earlier, it was none of her business. But she couldn't get Whitney's sly looks and overly affectionate actions out of her mind. She didn't trust the conniving woman.

Megan closed her eyes and nestled down in the bed, shifted her head in the plump pillow, and sighed. Egypt. She was in Egypt. And what she'd seen so far was a far cry from what she'd expected—modern city streets, busy squares, and buildings against the ancient backdrop of side streets with people selling their wares on every corner. Storefronts with garage-type doors opening to small rooms set up to sell clothes and spices were everywhere. A variety of small coffee shops where men hung out throughout the day and enjoyed tobacco from their *Shisha*—a gurgling water pipe for smoking tobacco—a scene right out of Arabian Nights. Even the chaotic traffic didn't detract, it only added to the enchantment of Cairo.

Megan fell asleep listening to *Isha*—the evening call to prayer.

****

Jordan tossed and turned. The Islamic call to prayer had ended and his mind was still bogged down on his bad luck. The 1,000-count-Egyptian-thread cotton sheets tangled in his legs. He yanked at them, kicked at them with his feet, pounded his pillow, and threw his hands over his head. How was he going to manage to keep his distance from Whitney Nash and concentrate on the conference, the team's contract proposal, and making tenure? Was it his unfortunate fate in life that he should be constantly reminded of the past? He'd done nothing wrong. How was he ever going to live the false accusation down and find someone who wouldn't hold it against him? Someone to love him for real? And it hadn't helped when that she-devil Whitney Nash had shown up today. Bringing back all the horrific scenes he thought he'd managed to overcome. Natalie, his fiancée, had called him a sexual predator. Even his female students had kept a wide berth after his return from a semester's leave of absence. Which of course had been a relief—he'd been able to concentrate on his teaching.

And now, even Megan shied away from him.

With his love life non-existent, he'd focused on his teaching and extension career, and making tenure. But when Megan walked out of her bedroom earlier, into the main room of their suite in a knock-out of a low-cut, black dress she'd worn to perfection, he was bowled over. If he hadn't bought that flimsy scarf for her, something to cover up her delectable skin that cried out to be touched, he'd have had a hard time keeping his hands off her all night. As it was, almost every guy at the reception hadn't been able to keep their eyes off her. Her ginger, pixie haircut combined with her barely there dress that accentuated her every petite feminine curve had his other head paying attention. Just getting by on a daily basis with Megan Holloway at his side was going to be a trial.

It was going to be hell.

Shit. She'd made him feel like a heel taking her away from an ailing mother. If it had been his mother, or any close member of his family, he'd have refused to leave their side until they were well out of harm's way. He pounded the pillow with his left fist, and slid the other hand underneath, then laid his head back down. On top of everything else, Megan must be beside herself with worry trying to keep her mind on her job while her mother was lying in a nursing home. Well, Helen said she was an extremely organized, responsible person. Still, he was going to have words with Helen the next time they talked.

****

Megan was in awe of the large breakfast buffet island laden with fresh dates, figs, pineapple, sliced oranges, apricots, various cheeses, strips of lamb and chicken, stewed tomatoes, and eggplant. There were the usual eggs, yogurt, breads, and bowls of prepared *umm Ali*—the Egyptian version of bread pudding layered with nuts and raisins. She couldn't resist starting her meal with the bread pudding to go with her coffee. Spoon in midair, she was about to savor another mouthful of the tasty concoction soaked in cream when Jordan and Dr. Omar Nagid's conversation caught her attention.

"I contacted the men in charge of your father's dig in Luxor this morning," Dr. Nagid said. "Apparently there has been an accident—a couple of young interns sustained serious injuries. Two American students fell from a scaffold. One broke his leg and the other his wrist. Both suffered contusions and were taken to Luxor Hospital, and then flown back to New York."

"What about the others? My father? My brother?" Jordan's eyes were riveted on Dr. Nagid's in anticipation of his answer.

"I was assured both your father and brother Caleb are unharmed. They are anticipating your visit when you arrive in Luxor."

Jordan's relief was visible as he lifted his coffee cup to his tight lips. Megan's interest, on the other hand, was piqued by the mention of the excavation site in the arid Egyptian desert. She immediately envisioned images of the Indiana Jones movies as Jordan and Dr. Nagid continued to discuss the situation in which Jordan's father was involved. She sipped her coffee, enthralled, her head bobbed between the two, her attention captivated once again by the mention of Luxor and the Valley of the Kings. Would she have an opportunity to visit King Tut's tomb? If she recalled, there was much interest in the current research. Something about hidden chambers and possible connection to Queen Nefertiti's burial close by. Too bad there hadn't been time to do extensive research on Egypt's history before leaving New York.

"Miss Holloway, I understand you are here to protect our ancient relics," Dr. Nagid said, bringing her out of her musings. "It is good to see someone is on board to keep our American friends cognizant of our heritage. My country thanks you."

Megan smiled at the pleasant Egyptian. "In the course of working with Jordan and Greg to determine the best methods to incorporate without damaging the soil and surrounding people, I will do my best to make sure our team doesn't harm or disturb any antiquities they uncover. Let me know if there are specific issues we should be aware of while we visit the local farmers."

"I have compiled a list of important facts and protocol to heed while visiting our growers. I will hand it out at the conference later this morning. I will make sure you receive a copy."

"I look forward to reviewing it."

"Megan is good at what she does,' Jordan stated. "I'm confident she won't let you or the Egyptian government down."

Jordan's assurance to Dr. Nagid on her behalf was heartening. On the other hand, the pressure to perform her duties just became more stressful. She'd have to remain levelheaded with her eye on the job in order to live up to Jordan's confidence in her abilities.

"Yes, well, there is talk that several of the more priceless artifacts that were unearthed near your father's dig have gone missing," Dr. Nagid informed them. "I hope your father is not involved."

Jordan's shoulders shot back, his eyebrows raised as he returned Dr. Nagid's stare. "I doubt my father would have anything to do with such an underhanded plot to steal your antiquities. I hope the authorities recover the missing artifacts? Do they have any leads as to who is behind this?"

"Not at the moment, no. They are watching your father's dig carefully, as they are others, as well. A new site has been uncovered in the Valley of the Kings where much looting has been carried out over the years. There is money to be made on the open market. Let's hope they can recover our national treasures."

"I agree. I hope they locate them before they are lost forever."

Dr. Nagid finished his coffee, replaced his cup in the porcelain saucer, and excused himself.

"It is time to prepare for the morning sessions. Please, don't get up. I will see you later."

Megan and Jordan finished their meal in silence, and then joined the others in the auditorium for the first of the conference talks.

****

The morning session ended on a high note. Jordan had a better idea of what he was up against as far as the contract was concerned. He was confident their proposal stood a better than average chance of being chosen. He met with Greg and Megan for lunch and discussed the afternoon's schedule. They had made the decision to split their team between the two groups that had formed—Greg would go with the leader of group one, and he and Megan would join the second group.

The pre-arranged buses pulled into the circular drive in front of the hotel and stopped several feet in front of the crowd that had gathered. Jordan stepped aside to wait for Megan to join him. He scanned the participants boarding the first bus and spotted Whitney. True to form, she was following Dr. Nagid on to the first bus, giving him her saucy smile that lit up her face—and Dr. Nagid's. Jordan shook his head and sighed as the Egyptian gave her a helping hand on to the bus, then followed closely behind. The Egyptian didn't know what he was in for if he fell for her sexy deceit. Her pretty face, sexy body, and calculating mind spelled trouble. He spotted Greg's frowning look and nodded. Greg returned the nod, shook his head, and stepped onto the first bus, as well.

Jordan moved to the side as Megan approached and let her precede him on to their bus. They each accepted a bottle of water the bus driver handed out to everyone as they boarded, as well as a pamphlet with a list of the day's farm stops.

"You take the window seat—enjoy the view. Be sure to take notes of anything significant. You did bring your camera, didn't you?"

"It's in my bag."

"Good. If you need another disk or battery, let me know. I've stocked up."

"I'm set for now, thanks. Is there anything in particular you want me to take pictures of?"

"No. Just enjoy. We'll follow the Nile for a bit, and then veer off into the productive delta fields, according to the itinerary. Pretend you're a tourist."

"I'm beginning to feel like one." She slipped her shoulder bag strap over the hook on the back of the seat in front of her and retrieved her camera.

Her leg touched his, and he lost track of what he'd intended to say.

"Go ahead and act the tourist. Enjoy the experience while you can," he said instead, and then placed his water bottle in the seat pocket in front of him, sighed, and looked up as a few stragglers made their way down the aisle to their seats.

"I've not had the opportunity, or the funds, to travel. This is a first. It's a bit overwhelming."

"As you know, I plan to visit my father's dig while we're in Luxor. If you'd like, you can come along. Give you a chance to see history in the making."

"Oh, my God. You mean like an Indian Jones kind of excavation dig?"

"Not quite." He laughed. "But close. Nothing so exciting, I'm afraid. It's a rather dull, tedious career— until you find something worth the effort of spending hours digging. The media and TV shows have romanticized it. Perhaps we can get my father to give us a tour of the Valley of the Kings, as well. I haven't seen it, although I understand the long tunnel walls leading down into King Tut's chambers are lined with hieroglyphs and bas-relief, which many do find romantic. Many of the other tombs in the Valley of the Kings are also lined with well-preserved colorful ancient hieroglyphs."

The bus inched out into the traffic, the sun shone through the window, casting a glow over Megan's short pixy hairdo and her creamy complexion as if to highlight her being. She looked like an angel reflected in the windowpane. He wished he read auras. He would love to interpret the dreamy expression in her emerald eyes. She emitted a soft sigh a fraction of a second before she turned to look out the window and lifted the camera in preparation of taking photos. He hoped she wasn't going to be disappointed at his father's site. Although, it would be just like his father to make the whole archeological dig sound like a fantasy come to life, as usual.

****

Megan's view of Cairo was mixed. Once past the tall, impressive modern buildings set against a bustling city life like any other big city, the bus deviated and took them past the older section of Cairo—narrow streets littered with people walking, riding bicycles, motorbikes, and driving small cars. Tiny store fronts laid their wares out on a blanket on the congested sidewalks—an assortment of shoes, produce, spices, scarves—the variety endless. People in all manner of garb were going about their business. Although many people were dressed in Western clothing, an equal number of men were dressed in the native long sleeved collarless, long flowing *gallibaya* in varying shades of white, brown or gray, and sported loose scarves and white turbans. Women wore loose *tob sebleh* dresses with wide trousers called *tshalvar* which were gathered below the knee and fell to their ankles, while others sported a large rectangular *melaya luf* wrap made of black fabric as a modest cover worn over their shoulders in which they carried their purchases. Megan spotted several women swaddling their babies in these wraps. Other women carried on the tradition of wearing the long rectangular face veil *bur`a*. Once again she was enthralled at the colorful, chaotic, and intriguing scenes. Her camera at the ready, she couldn't resist capturing the street scenes, the vendors peddling their make-shift storefronts on wheels selling fresh fruits and vegetables along the highway.

If Jordan talked to anyone on the bus, she wasn't aware. She was in her own world, soaking up the ambiance and taking pictures at every turn. When they left the city behind and entered the rich fields of the Nile Delta, Megan was surprised at the lush greenness of the fields, palm trees, and the many canals built to divert the river and irrigate the fields. In the distance to the left was hot, dry sand, and nothing but desert for as far as the eye could see. The contrast was striking, bold, and enchanting.

Time flew by as they were taken deeper into the country. Anxious to tour the area with Jordan, Megan was frustrated when Whitney waved them down the minute they stepped from the bus at their first stop.

"I was hoping to meet up with you, Jordan. I hoped we could catch up, exchange ideas as we inspect the fields and view the techniques they use—get your take on things."

Whitney latched on to Jordan's arm and practically pulled him toward the front of the group, not giving him a chance to refuse. Caught up in the group of twenty other conference-goers, Megan hung back not wanting to get involved in whatever scheme Whitney had up her sleeve. She'd barely escaped being caught up in her scandal back in college. She didn't understand why Jordan was letting himself be entangled with her again. On the other hand, as long as it didn't affect her and her chances of receiving a good review at the end of two weeks, she could look the other way.

The remainder of the field tours continued in much the same manner as the first one—from Damanur to

Mansura, then on to Zagazig. At each location the focus was the same—talks of implementing a program that would enhance yield through sustainable development. Food security with an emphasis on quality and environmental safety was also highlighted. Megan made notes while Whitney continued to latch on to Jordan, followed him around the grower's fields, and made sure they were standing next to the speakers. Megan hung back not wanting to get caught up in Whitney's web. On occasion she'd catch a glimpse of Jordan and Whitney as they smiled at each other, laughed, with heads bent over a sample the growers were discussing. Real cozy.

Megan sat next to Jordan on the bus in between site visits. He was quiet, almost withdrawn, not sharing any of his findings. She continued to click pictures out the window, take more notes, and assumed they'd discuss it later in the evening when they returned to the hotel. As Greg had stayed with the first group, she was sure he'd have something to add to their own findings.

The afternoon dragged on with no time to stop to visit the pyramids. The drive back was long and tiring. Megan was ready to call it a night as soon as they returned to the hotel and finished their evening meal. Greg and Jordan, however, insisted they discuss the day's findings. Jordan invited Greg to join them in their suite.

"We meet the team at four o'clock tomorrow afternoon. Our flight to Luxor isn't scheduled until seven," Jordan reminded her, as Greg followed them into their suite.

Greg tagged the easy chair, leaving Megan and Jordan to share the sofa.

"We'll have plenty of time in the morning to visit the pyramids if you'd like." Jordan leaned forward, elbows resting on his knees. "We can pick up a tour from the hotel."

Jordan must have read her mind again. Now that she was in Egypt she longed to see as much of the ancient sites as time permitted. And that included the pyramids and Sphinx.

"I'd like that. Thanks."

"What about you, Greg? You up for a bit of touring?"

"No thanks. My talk, as you know, is scheduled for one o'clock, so I'll skip the tour to make sure everything is in order. Besides, I've had the honor of visiting them before." He turned to Megan, "Make sure he gets you up on a camel."

"Not a chance." She laughed. "Just seeing the pyramids up close will be an experience. What about the conference? Aren't there morning sessions we should attend?"

"Nothing we need to worry about," Jordan said. "After our findings this afternoon, I can see we'll have to break our project down into the various agro-ecological zones."

Jordan unbuttoned his shirt, reclined, crossed his right leg over his left knee, and rested his arm along the ridge of the sofa in her direction. Megan gulped, and turned her attention toward Greg, trying to concentrate on what he was saying.

"There are ten regional stations broken down into specific research, extension and training centers, too," Greg said. "If we can define the individual needs of each of the delta regions, we might have a better chance of obtaining the contract. I'll sit in on a couple of the other talks in the morning to see if there is anything we've missed."

Jordan's fingers, mere inches from her neck, exuded a heat that made it hard for Megan to concentrate on the conversation. She inched toward the end of the sofa and leaned forward in an effort to put distance between them, but there was little room to navigate.

"Greg will be able to ascertain the needs surrounding Aswan, while we cover Luxor over the next few days." Jordan yawned, ran his fingers through his rich sable hair, uncrossed his legs and leaned forward.

Megan felt his leg stretch out next to hers. She straightened and stood.

"I don't know about you two, but it's been another long day and I'm beat."

"I agree." Greg stood as well and strode to the door. "Have a good night, and a fun morning playing tourist."

"Let us know if you learn anything more at the conference." Jordan followed Greg to the door.

"I'll see you after lunch so we can catch up before our meeting."

Megan jumped at the opportunity to say goodnight and headed to her room. As soon as Greg shut the door behind him, Jordan had other ideas and waylaid her before she reached her bedroom door.

"Wait a minute. I'd like to have a word, if you don't mind. I think we need to discuss the Whitney Nash situation."

"It doesn't involve me. Whatever relationship you choose to have with her is between the two of you."

"You're wrong. There is no relationship between us, regardless of how she acts or what she might say. And there never was anything between us—ever! I want to make that clear up front."

"Thanks for sharing, but again, it doesn't concern me."

"I know a lot of people believed her accusations. It's true she rode with me to visit growers' sites, but we were never alone—there was always someone else in the vehicle with us. When we stopped for meals, it was always in a group."

"Really, Jordan, you don't have to explain. I believe you. Everyone in the dorm knew what Whitney was like back then. We were as shocked as you were when she filed that sexual harassment complaint. It couldn't have been easy for you."

"That's an understatement. You have no idea what I went through. My own fiancée didn't believe me and ended our relationship overnight. And, it ruined any potential relationship I initiated. Once they discovered my background, they dumped me as if I actually did time."

She had known he was engaged at the time but hadn't heard that his fiancée had broken it off. He'd kept his personal life to himself, which was the way it should be.

"Look, I'm sorry. And I'm sorry she showed up at the conference. However, from where I was standing it didn't look as if you were trying to distance yourself from her today." Okay, maybe she shouldn't have voiced her observation, but it was true. Even Greg was surprised Jordan wasn't pushing Whitney away.

He hung his head and stuck his hands in his slack's pockets.

"I'm sorry I mentioned it. You're right. It isn't something you should have to deal with. As far as trying to distance myself from her, I'm trying to keep things on a professional level. I don't want to upset her and have her cause another commotion or cause us to lose out on obtaining this contract. Not to mention I'm up for tenure. Somehow, she found out and mentioned it when we met last night. I don't trust her not to somehow put a monkey-wrench in our chances of obtaining this contract. I need to keep an eye on her, if you know what I mean?"

"Yes, but leading her on isn't going to help your situation. In fact, it will only make her more upset when you end the relationship."

"I repeat, there is no relationship. I am not leading her on."

"If you say so."

"Look, why I'm discussing this with you is…, well…, I wondered if you would intervene whenever you see the two of us in a situation you think needs interrupting. That way she won't think I'm the one putting up walls between us, so she won't get upset with me."

"So I'm to play the third wheel so to speak?"

"Well, if you put it that way, it just might work."

He didn't know what he was asking of her. She knew Jordan wasn't a sexual predator, that it had been Whitney's way of getting even with him for not giving her the grade she assumed she deserved.

"No promises. My main focus is this project. I want this contract as much as you."

"You're right, of course," Jordan said. "I'm sorry I mentioned it. Forget it."

"I'll do what I can to help, only because I know what a witch Whitney can be. Be careful, Jordan. I truly don't trust her."

"Neither do Greg and I. Between the three of us, we need to be alert. I'm not sure if she'll be going to Aswan or Luxor, so we'll have to wait and see. She isn't about to give up until she gets what she wants, and she wants that contract."

Megan figured what Whitney really wanted was Jordan.

Chapter Seven

Arriving at the entrance to the Giza Necropolis was nothing short of amazing. From a distance, the individual pyramids appeared tiny, perfectly triangular, and smooth. Up close, they revealed an altogether different contour—the individual blocks of stone stood out in relief. Although signs forbade climbing on the mammoth structure, several tourists had climbed the first few tiers to take selfies.

Walking from the tour bus across the hot desert sand toward the first and largest pyramid, Megan was glad she had worn sneakers. Having hot grainy particles sift between her toes would have been uncomfortable had she worn sandals. Jordan wore sneakers as well, and together they made their way toward the Pyramid of Khufu.

"History lesson number one," Jordan said as they neared the pyramid. "King Khufu, or Cheops, was from the Fourth Dynasty. His is the northern most pyramid, and largest of the three—approximately 148 meters. If you look up at the tip you can see it has lost its pointed peak."

"You seem to be well versed in Egyptian history." Megan tented hands over her eyes to shield the brilliant sun as she peered through sunglasses toward the tip of the pyramid Jordan indicated.

"When you have a father like mine, it comes naturally. He wanted me to become an archeologist and work with him like my brother, Caleb. As much as I considered it, my true interest was in agriculture."

"Well, I can't wait for lesson two." She looked at him, her brows rose, waiting to learn more about the site she was fortunate to be visiting.

"Come on. Let's check out the other pyramids."

They walked around the massive historic triangular structure. Other conference participants in their group had spread out and gone their separate ways.

"The second pyramid contains King Khafre's burial chambers. It's a bit shorter than Khufu's." Jordan continued, and then pointed toward the next pyramid. "And of course, King Menkaure's is much smaller at only 66 meters tall."

"Still, it's an amazing accomplishment for the time period they were constructed." Megan rounded the corner of King Menkaure's pyramid and came face to face with a camel decorated with colorful blankets tucked under an impressive saddle. Head ornaments, beaded tassels, and braided ropes completed the ensemble. An Egyptian in a long white cotton tunic clung to the camel's rope, a wide smile under his turbaned head.

"Ah, would you like to take a ride?" Jordan asked, an even wider grin on his face than the camel owner's smile. Jordan's sexy dimples winked at her. "You might not get another chance."

Megan cranked her head back and peered at the tall imposing camel's hump towering toward heaven. The long box-like saddle in varying shades of aqua, ruby, emerald, and amber covered the single hump.

Stretching from the front to the back of the animal, it appeared huge, intimidating, and definitely too far off the ground for her piece of mind.

"I'll pass, thank you."

"An experience not to be missed. I'll join you—keep you from falling off."

Without waiting for her consent, Jordan conversed with the gentleman whose smile now extended from ear to ear in invitation as he instructed the camel to bend its front knees. The animal kneeled, and then settled in a comfortable position on all fours, kicking up the white sand as he settled. Megan looked over the saddle—at least twenty other camels waited in varying states of readiness, also decorated in bright colors, and all being tended by men dressed in similar garb to the one in front of them. A few already had tourists saddled and were being lead into the wide expanse of desert far beyond the pyramids.

"After you." Jordan smiled. He took her hand and led her toward the cud-chewing passive animal. "It's like riding a horse. I'll be right behind you."

"Thanks, but I've never ridden a horse."

"We'll have to rectify that, as well. Shift your left leg over the saddle and slide into place."

Once in the saddle, Megan inched forward, clung to the saddle horn for dear life, her knuckles turning white. She gasped as Jordan slipped in behind her and positioned himself so close against her she could feel the tightness in his abs, the firmness of his thighs as they practically wrapped around her hips. His muscular arms enclosed her as if in a lover's embrace. Her breath caught and it had nothing to do with her acrophobia. Did he have any idea how his closeness, once again, aroused emotions deep inside better left buried in the desert sand?

The camel shifted, its long legs straightened in the front, then the back. They were jostled about, and if it weren't for Jordan holding her steady, she was sure she would have tumbled off. Shifting from side to side, more like rocking, her backside rubbed against Jordan's front. Her thoughts no longer centered on fear of heights. Her thin, gauzy top did nothing to protect her against the heat now scorching her insides—which had nothing to do with the scorching heat from the blazing sun.

Proceeding at a slow, steady pace, Megan relaxed and let the experience take hold—a cloudless azure sky above, white shimmering sand beneath, ancient pyramids in the background, and in the arms of one sexy man. The urge to lean her head into his chest and give in to a daydream of what Jasmine must have experienced on that flying carpet ride with Aladdin, was suddenly interrupted when the sound of pounding hoofs on the sand snapped Megan out of her contemplations. She turned in time to see Whitney approach at a reckless speed, waving like a madman, putting on a show. Leave it to Whitney to ruin the moment. The minute the vixen galloped up alongside them, Megan stiffened. She'd been riding high, encased in Jordan's arms, but now her spirits plunged.

"Jordan," Whitney called with a sexy giggle as if she were a teenager calling attention the captain of the football team. The woman wore confidence and sex appeal like her birthday suit. Scantily dressed, she looked like an extra on an Indian Jones movie.

There was no competing with someone like Whitney Nash—Megan didn't care if Jordan had intimated he wasn't interested in the woman the night before. It was more than obvious the witch wasn't about to let her desire to reclaim Jordan's affections go anytime soon.

"I'll race you." Whitney smiled. The devil-may-care twinkle in her eyes made it a challenge most men couldn't refuse.

"Another time, perhaps." Jordan's words sounded as if he were disappointed. "We were just about to turn around—we have a few other sites to visit this morning. We'll see you back at the conference."

"Suit yourself." Whitney grinned, nudged her camel forward, and took off, dust kicking up in her wake.

Megan's once in a lifetime adventure had just come to an end. She bent her head and covered her face with her shirt sleeve to keep from swallowing sand granules left in Whitney's wake. Jordan yanked on the ropes and the camel turned toward the group of tourists waiting their turn for a camel ride. His arm tight around her middle, she swayed into his chest as the camel changed directions.

"You okay?" he asked.

His breath stirred the wisps of hair at her temple. She shivered, clung to the saddle horn, and vowed never to ride a camel again. Or be this close to Jordan Kaine.

"I will be when I get off this animal."

"You did good, Meg."

Meg? He was calling her Meg now? Oh, her heart was in trouble.

Getting off the camel wasn't any easier than getting on. Jordan dismounted like a pro, and then offered his hand. She latched on to his strong grip for dear life and swung her left leg over the right side of the camel—and slid down—right into Jordan's sturdy, waiting arms. Her legs shook and she wasn't altogether sure it had anything to do with the jarring camel ride.

"Steady. Take a couple steps to get your land legs," he instructed, not letting go, his hands lingered on her shoulders. She was finding it hard to breathe.

"I'm fine. Really."

"As long as we're here, we might as well visit the Sphinx. It's part of the funerary complex of the Khephren Pyramid. We have plenty of time before we have to return to the hotel for lunch, and our meeting."

Megan, focusing on the Sphinx in the distance, put space between them. "I'd love to see the Sphinx up close. Lead the way."

The long leonine body of the Sphinx with its royal head, wearing the nemes-headcloth, false beard, and Uraeus serpent, and made of native limestone, was missing part of the face, including the nose and beard. It certainly didn't detract from the historic significance or the massiveness.

"The Sphinx is said to represent the god Horemahet from the 18th Dynasty. It's the oldest and largest specimen of its kind."

Jordan's words reinforced what she'd researched on the internet before breakfast that morning. It was more enticing to hear all about it while standing in front of the real deal. Standing on the walkway across from it, the desert and pyramids in the background, it was like a moment out of time. After several long minutes drinking it all in, she retrieved her camera and took several pictures. Caught up in her own world, she plummeted back to earth when Jordan touched her shoulder.

"If you're done taking pictures, give me the camera and I'll take one of you in front of the Sphinx with the pyramids in the distance."

It was the first time he'd offered to take a picture of her, and she jumped at the chance at having one to savor.

"Thanks." She handed him the camera.

When he was about to take the shot, Ruth, one of the women Megan had met from the conference stepped forward and offered to take a picture of the two of them together. Jordan raised his eyebrows at Megan, in question.

"Why not?" She didn't want to appear rude or make a big fuss in front of everyone else who was also lining up to take pictures.

Jordan handed the camera to Ruth, joined Megan, and wrapped his arm around her waist—his body pressed against the entire length of hers. Megan forced a bright smile despite the tingling sensations flooding her insides at his touch.

Hopefully, their accommodations in Luxor tonight wouldn't include a suite.

****

Jordan settled in his seat next to Salah on the small aircraft bound for Luxor later that evening. Megan sat in the seat behind them, giving Jordan the breathing space, he so badly needed after the morning they had shared. The camel ride with Megan was a mistake. The smell of her shampoo, body lotion, and her sexy spiked hair tendrils tickling his nose had set his nerve-endings on notice. And her sexy white silky gauzy long-sleeved loose top she wore did little to hide her smooth skin as she'd leaned into him. She had to have sensed the emotions coursing through his body. Dammit. It didn't help his resistance any when he'd stood next to her to have their picture taken in front of the Sphinx. Although he didn't regret the experiences, there would be no more close encounters like the ones today—he'd make sure of it. From here on out, it was all business. Only business. He had too much to lose.

He opened his laptop and buried himself in his work while Salah did the same. The findings of the day revealed nothing outstanding from their research so far. He shut his laptop, sat back, and wondered how Megan was handling the flight. Had she taken any Dramamine? Was she hanging on to the seat in a death grip, her eyes—those emerald green eyes—shut tight waiting to land already?

Jordan took a deep breath and let it out in a whoosh. Only business, he told himself. Only business.

"So, Salah, what do you make of the meeting with the delegation this afternoon?" Jordan asked the Egyptian sitting next to him.

"Ah. I am not clear. At first I thought you had the contract wrapped up, as you say. Then, it sounded as if the team from Germany was in the running."

"I agree. What do you think we need to do better to clinch the deal? My team is ready to work with the Egyptians to help the farmers improve their produce in the upper Nile Delta."

"They appeared to be agreeable with your plan in that region. It's the talk Dr. Sampson gave. It didn't do much to address the region around Aswan and Luxor. Perhaps your research in those regions over the next two days will shed some light on your program. It is wise you and Dr. Sampson have agreed to cover separate areas to further your analysis."

"I hope you're right. We have another meeting with them when we return to Cairo. If everything goes well, we'll be prepared. Thank you so much for your help. Your support of our project goes a long way to ensure our position over the others."

"I have listened to the other talks—your proposal makes sense for our country. Having Miss Holloway on your team is an advantage—a very smart move on your university's part."

Jordan knew that having a representative from Wild and Wonderful on the team was a bonus. But he wasn't so sure having Megan on the team was good for his personal peace of mind.

It was a short flight, and once they landed at the Luxor International Airport and checked into their hotel along the *Shari Kornesh El Nile* and the river, Jordan couldn't help be a bit disappointed when he discovered he and Megan weren't sharing a suite as they had in Cairo. They did, however, have connecting rooms.

"The field bus will be waiting for us at eight tomorrow morning," he informed Megan. "I'll meet you in the lobby. If you need anything in the meantime, just knock. Make sure you wear your field shoes. We'll be traipsing through sugar cane, and even though it's mostly arid countryside around here, we are closer to the Nile and there will be several canals transporting water to the crops. It'll be marshy, so there might be a few snakes."

"*Snakes!* There won't be any crocodiles, too, will there?"

Her face paled, and he immediately wanted to kick himself for being so insensitive.

"We have guides. You'll be fine."

She didn't look as if she believed him.

"Seeing as I'm here to take soil samples and help you with your research, I've done a bit of homework on the Nile since I arrived. I know ancient Egyptians considered the crocodile a god named Sobek. In fact, they used to keep crocodiles in pools and adorn them with crystals and gold earrings, and bracelets on their forepaws. Are you telling me there are none to be found along the river today?"

"I'm sure we'll be safe. And my father will be proud you took the time to brush up on your history and Egyptian lore. If I know him, he'll try to teach you how to read all those hieroglyphics on every temple in Egypt before you leave."

"I doubt it. Besides, I won't be here long enough."

"Too bad, I think you'd enjoy it. You seem to have fallen in step with the country in just a few short days."

"What's not to like. It's a very historic, picturesque, and an intriguing culture."

"I agree. So, relax. Settle in. I'll see you in the morning."

"Thanks. I think I'll call home and see how my mother is doing before I call it a night."

"Call me if you need anything."

****

The bus dropped them next to the Nile, Monday morning, along with a small contingent of people attending the conference and going on tour. Several feluccas waited close to shore, ready to take them to farms farther down river. Jordan, ever the gentleman, waited until Megan found a seat on the boat, and then sat next to her. To her chagrin, Whitney joined them, sitting on the other side of Jordan. Several Egyptians, including Mr. Delagad, who appeared to be leading their group, sat across from them. It looked as if Mr. Delagad and Whitney had become well acquainted over the past two days. The man couldn't keep his eyes off her. Not surprising the way she was dressed today—a red tank-top that emphasized her well-endowed breasts, thin waist, and a pair of tight black capris. Her stark-red shiny toenails peeked out from her toeless sandals. She swung her left leg over her right in his direction.

Megan shifted and gazed out over the water. She wrapped her simple, white, gauzy shirt around her melon t-shirt and tucked her feet, adorned with serviceable high-top shoes, under her seat, out of sight. Tall reeds lined the river bank. Water buffalo grazed a short distance beyond. Up ahead, a swarm of scantily dressed children frolicked in the water, and a rowboat waited close by.

Lost in wonder at the scenery surrounding them, Megan reached in her bag for her camera and was about to take a series of pictures of the enchanting scene along the shore when Jordan nudged her shoulder, drawing her attention back to the conversation in their boat.

"I can assure you we have done nothing of the sort," Jordan said, sitting back, eyebrows raised, looking at Megan as if seeking confirmation. "Whatever you've heard, Whitney, we are not the ones spreading such rumors."

Mr. Delagad's eyebrows rose as well, as he looked at Whitney. Megan had no idea what they were discussing, but it was obvious Jordan was being blamed for something. Whatever it was, Jordan was seeking her support.

"Jordan is right," Megan confirmed.

Jordan nodded his acknowledgment and glared at Whitney. "Where did you hear such a thing? And why would we spread such false rumors accusing you, or any of the others, of trying to undermine your chances of obtaining the contracts? We play fair, Whitney—we would never knowingly make bogus statements. Yes, we want the project, but we aren't going to be dishonest about it by spreading unfounded rumors. You of all people should know that about me."

Megan wanted to stand up and clap. Jordan had just put Whitney in her place, although it didn't bode well for their chances of winning the contract if Whitney had anything to do with it after Jordan's angry words.

"Jordan would never do such a despicable thing, Whitney. He's a very honorable man," Megan chimed in, despite Whitney's cynical look.

"Why, I really didn't think he would— intentionally. But what about you? Or Dr. Sampson? Otherwise, why would several project coordinators mention it to me in passing?"

"Again, I don't know where they got the notion we were targeting you in particular, but it simply isn't true," Jordan reiterated. "Whether it was myself, Megan, or Greg, it is all lies. I hope this puts an end to those rumors. We're all in this together and the Egyptian Government is going to decide who has the best feasible program that meets their needs, versus supposed rumors. At least I would hope that's the case."

"I am happy to know you are not guilty of such rumors, my friend," Salah Delagad spoke up in Jordan's behalf.

"Thank you. Our intent is to provide the best service to the Egyptian people," Jordan responded as the felucca docked alongside the bank of the Nile.

Megan didn't know what Whitney's game was, but Jordan was on the defensive. Something was brewing. And more than likely Whitney was behind it. Thankfully conversation was impossible as a large plank appeared and was placed between the boat and shore. Passengers stood and lined up to disembark along the make-shift platform. Mr. Delagad quietly escorted Whitney off the boat, and the two of them headed toward the small path along the bank where they all meandered toward a waving sugarcane field.

Had Whitney convinced Mr. Delagad that their character was questionable? Would it have a negative impact on their chances of gaining the contract?

The group spread out over the parameter of the field. Between taking soil samples, water samples, and plant strands, the researchers followed the path toward a narrow man-made canal and lined up along the bank. Not surprising, Whitney was suddenly at their side again, this time all smiles as if nothing had transpired on the felucca. Mr. Delagad headed the contingent, and led everyone toward a point closer to the river bank.

"What a glorious day for a farm visit." Whitney's about-face was saccharine—and false. "Luxor is such a charming place, don't you think? I'd love to explore one of the historic digs while I'm here. Oh, wait." She laid her hand on Jordan's arm. "I understand your father is here working on a project. Perhaps you can arrange a visit to his dig."

She didn't blame Whitney for wanting to see such an endeavor, but after the accusations on the felucca earlier, she wondered what Whitney was up to now.

"It's actually not far from here," Jordan said. "Any one of the conference coordinators can arrange a visit to the excavation site. However, the Egyptians are very concerned about visitors so you'll more than likely have a chaperone accompany you."

"Oh, come on. Your father is one of the archeologists. I hear he's heading up the project. Surely you have the influence to allow a few visitors to visit his site."

"I haven't met with him since arriving in Egypt. Talk with Mr. Delagad—see what he can arrange. Perhaps a few of the others would like to join you."

He was covering his ass. Good for him.

Whitney smiled as if she'd won a blue ribbon, then turned and made her way to the front of the group. Megan joined Ruth and a few of the others as they followed Mr. Delagad closer to the Nile. They walked toward one of the wider canals carrying much needed water into the field. Before they had gone several yards, a loud chilling scream filled the air. Megan froze. Her heart raced. Jordan, along with several of the men ran forward, while those already in the process of taking samples, stopped, and turned toward the commotion.

Oh, my God! Was it a crocodile? Had someone been attacked? Her mind raced, she couldn't breathe. The crowd drew closer to the edge of the canal bank.

Megan held back. What she was able to observe from her vantage point behind the others made her head spin—a body!

Before she realized it, Jordan was at her side. He wrapped his arm around her shoulders and drew her into his warm, reassuring embrace. She clung to him in horror.

"Don't look," he whispered in her ear.

"What happened?"

"They found a body and are dragging it out of the canal. They think it is someone from a nearby dig."

Megan knees gave out. Jordan caught her, drew her closer, kissed her forehead, and with strong hands, set her aside. "I understand there has been trouble at my father's site not far from here. I want to go back and get a closer look—make sure the body isn't my father's, or brother's. There have been too many incidents lately at his excavation site in regards to more 'Westerners' being employed then locals. Let's hope this has nothing to do with my father's dig."

Megan hugged him, not wanting to be left alone standing in the middle of nowhere.

"Ruth," Jordan called over her shoulder. "Will you stay with Megan, please? The two of you don't need to see this. I'll be right back."

"Of course." Ruth rushed to Megan's side and led her away from the scene. Megan let her. Harold Smart, another conference attendee from England, joined them and found a dry spot in the field where others, including Whitney, had gathered to stay out of the way. They huddled in the lush expanse of sugarcane. No one spoke. Finding a dead body in a canal was mind-blowing to begin with—the implications were limitless.

Had this person tripped and drowned? Had he been pushed? Megan didn't want to think it might be Jordan's brother. She took several deep breaths. It seemed like forever before Jordan came back to report his findings.

"According to Salah, it looks as if it's a young American male—probably from one of the archaeological digs. The person they dragged from the canal was too young to be my father. And, thank God it was not my brother, Caleb." Jordan exhaled, brushed his hands over his face, and shook his head. "I need to check in with my father as soon as possible to make sure he and my brother are okay."

Chapter Eight

With the afternoon field visits cancelled due to the discovery of the dead body, the group was bused back to their hotel.

"I'm going to arrange transport to my father's dig, Megan. Would you like to come along?" Jordan leaned against the open connecting door between their rooms. He knew he shouldn't ask, shouldn't let her tag along. It could be too risky. But he needed to check on his father and brother to make sure they were okay and, since the afternoon tour had been rescheduled for tomorrow, it would make the next two day's schedule with little time to meet with his father before their return flight to Cairo. Megan had been looking forward to visiting an excavation site. With time on their hands, now, it was an opportunity to take advantage of their limited time in Luxor. And, honestly, he wasn't sure he wanted to let her out of his sight—for safety reasons, of course.

"Are you sure it will be okay on such short notice? I know you said such visits would have to be approved."

"I need to make sure my father and brother are okay. We can observe several of the fields along the way if it makes you feel better about going."

"In that case, I'd love to tag along."

"I'll call the front desk and make arrangements for transportation," he confirmed, then crossed the room to pick up the phone. "Make sure you put on plenty of sunscreen. As hot as it is along the river, it can be sweltering out in the desert."

"Jordan…"

He faced her, her expression unreadable.

"Thank you. For being there for me when they discovered the body. I'm glad it wasn't your brother."

"It wasn't easy on any of us. I'm glad it wasn't my brother, too. The fact that the body might be connected to my father's dig is troublesome."

"It made me think about how short life can be. It also reminded me I should call home again and check on my mother. I know Lindsey said she was doing okay. But I want to call the hospital this time just to make sure. Maybe talk to my mother."

"No problem. I understand. Go ahead and make your call."

"Thanks."

****

Megan's relief was tangible after talking to her mother before leaving the hotel. A heavy weight had lifted from her shoulders after hearing a positive tone in her mother's voice. For once her mother didn't send guilt waves over the phone. Megan was finally able to relax in regards to her mother's care since landing in Egypt and found herself looking forward to observing a real live Egyptian 'dig.'

Megan couldn't help but smile at the images depicted in front her as she and Jordan stepped from the somewhat dilapidated vehicle Jordan had hired. She was about to experience a real live historic Egyptian excavation site—up close and personal. Despite the morning's shocking events at discovering a dead body, her insides were bubbling with renewed excitement.

Steam rose from the arid sand in shimmering waves. The sun blazed overhead. In the distance, people worked the earth like ants tunneling through a hillside. They diligently carted small buckets of soil and dumped it away from the open pit. Others were bent over swiping brushes against the sides of the elongated hole in the ground. Locals dressed in flowing white garments worked alongside those dressed in tank tops and shorts. With no shade to be found, a large nomadic-style, elongated, open tent had been erected to the left of the site. Two tables, several camp chairs, and three blue coolers tucked under a table were centered underneath the canopy.

Her delight was short-lived, however as she sensed Jordan's tenseness when they neared the work area. He strode with purpose, his hands balled into fists, oblivious to her presence. The hot sand made it impossible to keep up with his hurried stride. Able to observe him undetected, he cut an impressive figure—dark hair mussed, aviator sunglasses hiding his expressive eyes, a tall, firm torso, muscular arms swinging at his sides, and a pair of Dockers that only enhanced his strong legs—an image right out of GQ. Her heart skipped a dozen beats as she took it all in and recalled his kiss at the canal. It hadn't been a real kiss on the lips, but the endearment sent sparks clear to her toes. Did he even realize he had kissed her?

A loud booming shout rang out, drawing her attention to the team in the distance. Heads turned in their direction. Only one person stepped forward and ran toward Jordan with outstretched welcoming open arms.

"Son, what are you doing here?"

"Dad. I'm so glad to see you're okay."

Jordan ran toward his father and the two wrapped their arms around each other in a show of kindred affection. The display brought tears to Megan's eyes. Her insides warmed at the strong family ties as she witnessed father and son's genuine affection for each other. She was reminded of her own close ties with her mother, who she had almost lost a few short weeks ago. She wiped a stray tear from her cheek, and hung back, not wanting to interrupt their moment.

"Of course, I'm okay, son. Why wouldn't I be?" Henry Kaine patted his son on the back, then stepped to the side. His confused expression indicating he had no knowledge of the dead body that had been discovered along the canal that morning.

"We were touring a sugarcane field earlier today. A young man was discovered in a canal from an apparent drowning. They said it might be an intern from your dig."

"Oh, my, God! Caleb and Gabe left to go to town for supplies. They haven't returned. Did they identify the body?"

"No, but thank God it wasn't Caleb. When they stated it might be an American from a nearby dig, I made it a point to view the body. I wanted to make sure it wasn't either of you. I haven't heard any further details. They cancelled our tour for the afternoon, so we decided to check and make sure you and Caleb were okay."

Megan detected the concern in both their voices. If the men hadn't returned yet, where were they? If the body wasn't Caleb's, was it Gabe's?

Not wanting to interrupt, she remained silent until Jordan looked her way. It took a minute for him to focus and realize she was standing close by.

"I'm sorry, Megan. Let me introduce you to my father." He came to her then, took her hand and drew her to his side. "Dad, this is Megan Holloway from the Wild and Wonderful Corporation. She's part of our team. Megan, this is my father, Henry Kaine."

"Very pleased to meet you, young lady." Henry Kaine extended his hand, taking hers in a firm clasp. "I apologize for my son. I hope he has had better manners than he exhibited leaving you standing alone just now."

"He has. No need to apologize. I understand your concern."

"I must apologize again to excuse myself. I must talk to Omar—see if he has had news of the incident. If you would make yourself comfortable under the tent, I will arrange someone to show you around."

"I'll join you, Dad. I'm sure Megan will be okay on her own for a while."

His look was meant to reassure even though he raised his eyebrows above his sunglasses in question.

"Of course I can manage. You've got more important business to deal with then to worry about me. Go. I'll be fine. I can watch the dig in progress from beneath the tent, out of everyone's way. I promise. I'll be fine."

Henry Kaine beamed at her, nodded, and together father and son wasted no time searching out Omar. Megan headed for the tent—and the shade.

****

"What's going on, Dad? I'm thinking this dig is more dangerous than anything you've undertaken so far. What are you working on that is causing so much trouble?"

"Nothing we can't handle—a few minor mishaps, son, and until now it wasn't anything major."

"I don't buy that. Selah mentioned several Americans have been injured to the point they've been flown back home. That sounds major to me. And now this?"

"Okay, so I'm a bit worried. Yes, there has been some grumbling about there being too many 'westerners,' mostly American's, on the dig. And a few of the artifacts we've found have come up missing. Not sure who's been spreading the seed of dissent. Omar has been keeping communications open—keeping us informed as best he can. Apparently, there are a few who are afraid we are the ones absconding with whatever antiquities we discover instead of making sure the artifacts remain in Egypt, or that we'll get all the credit. I understand their concern. The entire team has been vetted. As far as I'm aware, there doesn't seem to be any connection to the smuggling ring that's been implicated in other cases, such as the one in Shanghai a few years ago. We are watchful, and all feel the same way here. Whatever we unearth stays right here in Egypt. We all get the credit."

"I'm beginning to think there is a connection to the conference," Jordan said. "There's been some talk about making sure the contracts go to a university other than ours. Someone is spreading rumors pitting us against other institutions vying for the contracts, which make us look bad."

"Let's hope you're wrong. In any case, keep your ears and eyes open, son."

"So, where is Omar? I talked with him the other day at the conference and understand he was going to be here this morning."

They had been walking while talking, their steps taking them past the dig as they headed for a large sand dune to the left. The sun blazed in the cloudless stark blue sky, the heat intense. Jordan couldn't help but smile as his father climbed the steep slope with ease. Nothing wrong with his father's stamina and grit—the man was in excellent physical shape for his age.

"Omar is over the ridge of this mound working on what we assume is the back portion of a boat that was unearthed while we were working on a different project—it's rather a long boat of sorts."

They reached the crest of the mound and scanned the area. Omar stood thirty yards away talking to another Egyptian dressed in a typical long flowing white robe, his head bound with a white turban. Taller than Omar, the man towered above, his stance menacing as if they were involved in a heated discussion. Omar straightened and stepped away, directed his gaze up at the gentleman as if ready to respond. However, the tall man spotted Jordan and his father, then shook his head at Omar, spoke, and walked away. Omar's immediate smile as he turned his attention to Jordan's father was forced, the corners of his mouth wobbly. Nevertheless, Omar threw up his arms in welcome as he walked toward them.

"My friend, what can I do for you?" Omar's greeting was cautious.

"There has been another accident," Jordan's father didn't waste time getting to the point. "This one, deadly—an American boy was found in a canal not far from here. What news do you have for me? My son Caleb and Gabe have not returned from the village yet. I'm concerned."

"I have just now received word. An unfortunate incident. An accidental drowning. Nothing more."

"Jordan was there when they found the body. Thank the Lord it wasn't my other son, Caleb. Like I said, neither he nor Gabe has returned from town with the new supplies."

"Not to worry. Be patient. They will return soon. You will see. I will go to town to see for myself what is happening."

"I appreciate your assistance. If you wish, I'll have the others start on the north end of the dig where we found the underground tunnel. Who knows, it may lead to another interesting find. Perhaps a burial site of some significance."

"Be careful my friend," Omar said in parting. "We don't want a cave-in or another major accident. I will see you when I return—hopefully with good news."

Omar turned and followed in the taller man's footsteps toward the back side of the sand dune before Jordan and his father turned and walked back to the dig in progress.

"Perhaps we should conduct our own investigation," Jordan said. "Find out what's keeping Caleb and Gabe."

"Knowing those two, they've more than likely stopped off at one of their favorite eating haunts for some decent food."

"Still, you should check it out—make sure the body they found wasn't Gabe's."

"You're right. Let me make sure things are going okay here before we leave."

Jordan's father left to make the necessary arrangements with his team while Jordan went in search of Megan. As he neared the tent a small motor coach pulled up. No sooner was the engine shut off, then the doors slid open and a stream of conference attendees alighted. Jordan spotted Whitney as she stepped from the bus—hard to miss with her chartreuse sun dress, matching wide-brimmed sun hat, sun glasses, and skimpy, strappy sandals. Whitney waved, drawing attention to herself as usual.

Shit. Now what was she up to?

****

Megan pursed her lips as the small bus stopped alongside the tent and Whitney Nash exited in her stylish flare as if she was the star of the desert. Ruth and Harold were among the others from the conference who eagerly alighted, smiles of excitement evident when they spotted her.

"Everyone please gather under the tent before we get started." A young Egyptian pointed as if they needed directions to the tent. He stood off to the side waiting for the last person to exit the bus.

Whitney waved and called out to Megan as she paraded by, "I see Jordan brought you along—how cozy."

Her tone snide, the witch turned to Ruth and smiled, her facial expression changed on a dime as she said, "Isn't this exciting?"

Megan didn't think Whitney needed or expected a reply. Ruth, however, waved back. As Whitney moved on with the others. Ruth was discreet enough not to comment on Whitney's snide remark.

"Have you had a chance to check things out yet?" Ruth asked as she turned from the group now gathered under the far end of the tent. "Harold and I were excited to pick up the tour at the last minute."

"I was waiting for Jordan and his father to come back. They went to talk to Dr. Nagid to see if he has heard anything about this morning's incident at the canal. It seems Jordan's brother, and an intern, haven't returned from town. Jordan's father is worried something might have happened to them and that the person they found might be one of the interns named Gabe."

"Oh, no! How horrible. Maybe this is a bad time for everyone to be visiting the dig?"

"It doesn't look as if the news has reached the site yet. You go ahead, I'll wait for Jordan. He should be back any minute."

"Oh, look, here he comes now." Ruth smiled in welcome as Jordan approached.

Before Jordan made it to where they were standing, Whitney waylaid him, wrapped her arm around his, and gazed up in to his face. Despite their sunglasses, Megan swore Whitney's eyes were fluttering up and down to beat the band. Jordan's reaction to Whitney was cool— her apparent attempt at flirting failing. His father's smile and instant awareness of the vixen, however, was priceless. Megan couldn't hear their exchange, but she smiled as Jordan disentangled his arm and moved away. Not to be outdone, Whitney turned her attention to the other men in the group and followed them under the tent canopy. Jordan then made his way to where Megan and Ruth waited. He stopped so close to Megan that she had to step back in order to look up at him when he spoke.

"I'm going to return to Luxor with Dad so he can identify the body—see if it's Gabe's. Ruth, is there room on the bus for Megan to catch a ride back to the hotel?" Jordan enquired.

"Yes, not everyone wanted to come, so there are a few extra seats. I'm sure it will be okay with our guide."

"Don't worry about me. I'll be fine," Megan assured him. "You do what you have to do. I hope the body isn't Gabe's. And I hope your brother is safe."

"Thanks. You ride back with the others and I'll meet you at the hotel for dinner."

Jordan placed his arm over Megan's shoulder, and slightly squeezed, his touch meant to be soothing. Instead, shivery tingles running down her arm, scorching straight to her inner core, did little to calm her growing desires where Jordan was concerned. Megan glanced over her shoulder to find Whitney's lowered eyebrows, scrunched forehead, and tight lips directed her way. Whitney turned and joined the others under the tent. Megan inhaled and let it out slowly. For two cents, she'd go back to town with Jordan and his father so she wouldn't have to deal with Whitney's surly attitude the rest of the afternoon.

"Son, I've made arrangements for Eric to escort the group around the excavation site. If you're ready, we can get going." Henry Kaine nodded at Megan and Ruth. "If you'll excuse us, ladies, I'm sure you'll be in good hands this afternoon."

Jordan gave her shoulder another tug, then turned and left with his father. Megan followed Ruth to the tent where the others waited for Eric to begin the tour.

"Maybe I shouldn't ask, and you can tell me it's none of my business, but are you and Jordan an item?" Ruth asked. "I've notice he's never far from your side and seems rather proprietorial."

As much as Megan wanted to tell her they were an 'item,' the truth was, she and Jordan weren't.

"No. He knows this is my first international travel assignment and being a novice, he feels protective."

"Too, bad. You seem like a perfect fit."

"That's because we agree on many of the aspects of this project. What about you and Harold?" Megan smiled as she changed the subject and put the ball in Ruth's court.

"I've known Harold a long time. He's married to his work. We're just friends."

Eric called the group to attention, putting an end to their conversation. He escorted everyone across the hot desert sand to a location where a young girl sat cross-legged with a drawing pad in her lap as she sketched the landscape. Another young man was drawing intricate details of several of the items that had been discovered in the area. Across the roped-off area, a photographer had set up his tripod and was filming as everyone went about the excavation process.

Megan panned the area with her camera, took in the vastness of the site, and had a field day taking pictures. The various people working on the dig reminded her of similar excavations in progress she'd only seen in movies. With the large golden sand hills in the background, and the azure sky high above, she couldn't resist taking one picture after another until she had to dig in her bag for a new disk.

As the group followed Eric, they drew closer to the actual dig where he instructed them to keep a safe distance from the work in progress so as not to disturb the area or fall into one of the pits. Young Egyptians worked alongside Westerners, slowly brushing sand aside, scraping, sifting, and picking through the findings. Megan took in the blazing sun high above, the scent of sand, sweat, and murmurs, and once again she envisioned images of Indiana Jones. Hats shadowed faces covered in sunscreen. She marveled at the concentration, the methodology, and patience needed to work on such an excavation under the extreme heat. The satisfaction of finding any artifact, no matter how small, must be exhilarating for the workers. She continued to take pictures as they were escorted among the activity.

Under the spell of her surroundings, Megan fell in step with the others when a shadow fell across her vision and an unmistakable fragrance filled the air. Whitney Nash. Before Megan could react and walk away, Whitney laid a hand on her arm.

"I'd like a word, Megan. I'm afraid we got off to a bad start."

Oh, Lord, here it comes. She'd been waiting for Whitney to corner her since her arrival in Cairo. Other than vying for the same contract, it was obvious Whitney had her eye on Jordan. To what end, she didn't have a clue. Whitney must be aware Jordan wasn't interested. Or was he?

"What can I do for you?" Megan focused on Whitney's demeanor, her facial expression. She didn't trust her—it was as simple as that.

"I want to apologize. Just so you know, I had nothing to do with those rumors about you and Jordan accusing me and a few of the others about pandering to the Egyptian Agricultural Ministry. In fact, I talked to Salah on your behalf."

Megan doubted she was on their side. After all, they were vying for the same contract.

"That's kind of you, Whitney. And I appreciate your efforts. To be clear, we did not speak badly of you or anyone else to the Ministry, or other dignitaries. I have no idea who started those rumors. However, it's neither here nor there at this point. The fact is, the Ministry will make their own decision based on the proposals submitted. I'm sure you'll be as thorough in your proposal as we will." Relieved to see Whitney was keeping their conversation on a professional level, Megan smiled. About to join the group, however, Whitney changed tactics with her parting shot.

"I'm sure Jordan will present a valid proposal— that is if he can keep his mind focused on the project instead of on you. Oh, look, the group has moved on. We must catch up or they'll leave us behind."

Before Megan could reply to Whitney's dig, she was left standing alone, wondering what Whitney had up her sleeve now.

****

"There was to be no killing," Salah Delagad said. "Did I not make it clear that I would not be involved in this scheme if anyone died—only injuries to scare off the Kaines." Salah wrung his hands and looked back and forth between the two men sitting across from him in the small tea shop on the outskirts of Luxor.

"What can I say? Accidents happen," Habib El-Said quipped and shrugged his shoulders. "It might not have been planned, but we can use it to our advantage, can we not?"

"I don't like it," Salah quipped back at the stern Egyptian.

"You cannot back out now," Omar Nagid spit out through clenched teeth, slapping his hand on the table.

There was no way Salah could back out without ending up dead, and in a location where they would never find his body. He had to play along. If he could keep his friends safe—no further deaths—he would do what he could until things came to a close.

"So, we will plan our next move," Habib said, clearly talking to Omar. Habib drank from his cup, brushed his dark mustache with his forefinger and thumb, and eyed Salah, eyebrows raised. "What is next on Jordan Kaine's agenda?"

Salah took a minute to drink from his own cup before answering. The afternoon conference was an open forum for anyone interested in knowing more about the international program going on here in Luxor.

"The conference participants are scheduled to partake of a hot air balloon excursion along the Nile early tomorrow to observe the fields from above. I understand Jordan Kaine and his assistant Ms. Holloway plan to participate."

"Are you accompanying them?" Omar asked Salah.

"No. I will remain at the conference to welcome those from Aswan later in the day. What are you two planning?"

"Nothing to concern yourself," Habib stated. "You keep your eye on those returning from Aswan by boat. We will keep a look-out for those sailing the skies tomorrow."

Habib and Omar shared a private smile. Salah didn't trust either one. Whatever the two were working on, at least he would try to be prepared. If he so much as thought about warning Jordan Kaine to be on the lookout for danger, and got caught, his own life would be the one on the line. The authorities on the other hand should be warned.

"Where is Henry Kaine, now?" Habib asked.

"I understand he is in town to identify the dead body from the canal. Imagine his surprise when he discovers one of his assistants—his son's cohort," Omar replied.

"By the way," Habib continued, "where is Kaine's son, Caleb?"

Salah kept to himself, there was no way he was going to let these two know where Caleb Kaine was located. At least Henry Kaine's son was safe, even though he had sustained injuries during the attack. Habib and Omar weren't the only ones who had secret contacts owing favors.

Chapter Nine

"Are you convinced now, Dad? It could have been Caleb instead of Gabe, or both of them." Jordon threw the accusation across the table like a dare. "How many more 'accidents' like this is it going to take before you and the others realize there is something going on?"

Henry Kaine ran his hand through his disheveled, wiry graying hair. He hung his head and shook it. "I know, I know. But I have no idea what or who is behind it. It could be anyone."

"When did these accidents start?"

"We've been here almost a month setting up for the excavation next to the hillside. We attributed the collapse of the scaffolding to the pocket of sand giving away. It had been erected too fast without making sure the foundation was able to hold the weight."

"At least those two survived. If this wasn't an accident, I'll eat my hat. We need to find Caleb."

"I alerted the authorities while you were in touch with your Ms. Holloway. They are investigating the incident. They plan to dredge the canal to see if there is another body."

Jordan let the inference of Megan being *his* Ms. Holloway go, but the mention of her name in connection with him tugged at his insides. Right now, he had to concentrate on his brother's safety—hope like hell he wasn't lying in a canal somewhere. In addition, he had to focus on obtaining the contract for the university. And yes, dammit, his tenure. Although if push came to shove, tenure wasn't exactly high on his list at the moment.

"Have there been arguments—dissention among the workers?" Jordan leaned back in the ladder-back wooden chair facing the entrance and scanned the small café. Used to keeping an eye on his students on the many field trips they'd taken, he'd always found it easier to sit in a location where he had the best advantage of the room and the main entrance to keep an unobtrusive eye on things. Not only could he check out the locals coming and going in the small café now, he would be in a position to make sure his father wasn't about to be the next victim of whatever the hell was going on.

And hopefully see his brother walk in unharmed.

"No. No dissention that I'm aware of," his father confirmed. "Everyone seems to be getting along, helping out, and volunteering to do what they can to get the job done. The excitement on this dig, with many of the young novices, has been encouraging. You know how boring, tiring, and disappointing these digs can be at times."

"So, where would Caleb hang out? What contacts has he made here in Luxor? There has to be something we can do besides sit on our hands while the authorities investigate the incident."

"I can check with the local growers where we purchase our fresh produce, and at the marketplace— see if anyone has seen him."

"It's a start. And I can check with some of the growers we visit. Someone must have seen something."

Jordan's attention turned to the two men from the conference that entered the café and took a seat on the other side of the room. No threat there. He nodded and smiled at them and turned back to his father.

"I have to get back to the dig and make sure everything is in order," his father said. "What's on your itinerary for tomorrow? I could squeeze in some time for a quick walk through of a couple burial sites in the Valley of the Kings if you aren't busy. They've had some new findings. We can check with the crews there to see if anything unusual has been going on at their end. Oh, and maybe your lady friend would like to come along?"

"Stop the match-making, Dad. You know where I stand on that issue. There is too much at stake with the contract negotiations, and my tenure, to get involved romantically right now. Besides, in case you haven't heard, the student who accused me of sexual harassment has shown up at this conference. In fact, you ogled her earlier when she arrived at your dig. I'm trying hard to keep her at bay, but she's starting to be a problem. She's been coming on to me and I don't want to upset her by coming right out and telling her to get lost, only to cause more problems."

"Point taken. So, invite Ms. Holloway, and anyone else along, and we'll make it a tour. Keep it small."

"We have an early morning hot air balloon ride along the Nile to observe the various fields from above. Not only a conference perk, but it will give us an idea of the scope of the entire area's growing region and canal systems. I'm pretty sure we have meetings after lunch. I'll recheck our itinerary and let you know. In the meantime, do you mind dropping me off at the hotel?

Greg is coming in from Aswan today, and we need to collaborate on his research findings from that region."

****

The riverboat from Aswan to Luxor arrived early afternoon. Jordan, Megan, and the other conference attendees had finished the organized evening meal and were filing in to the hotel conference center auditorium for the rescheduled seminar. Greg met up with them as Jordan ushered Megan down the center aisle.

"What is this I hear of another accident on your father's dig?" Greg asked. "How serious was it?"

"Serious enough. One of my father's assistants was found dead in a canal. My brother is missing, and the authorities are on the case."

"Whew! Hope your brother is okay."

"Thanks. How was Aswan?"

"Uneventful, but productive. We're on the right track. Nothing we haven't already considered in our proposal."

"Glad to hear it." Jordan indicated a row of seats with an advantageous view of the panel on the stage. He waited until Megan found a seat and then sat next to her, their shoulders lightly touching. Her Lotus Blossom fragrance surrounded him and filled his senses with erotic images.

"What about Luxor? Anything we should be concerned about here?" Greg interrupted his sensual musings.

Where to begin?

"You mean other than the incidents with the dig and cancelling the rest of the morning's field trips because of the discovery of the dead body? Whitney has intimated we're plotting against her. Seems

126

someone is spreading rumors against some of the others, as well, and suggesting Megan and I are the guilty culprits. Apparently, Whitney can't accept the fact I'm not falling under her spell—again. I suspect she is the one spreading the rumors to get even with me. You know I've bent over backward to play nice, Greg. It isn't working."

"That happened so long ago, why would she even care now?"

"Exactly. I don't know. Why did she target me in the first place?"

"Considered it would help her ace your class, maybe?" Greg chuckled, then changed the subject. "So what's on the agenda tomorrow?"

Jordan was glad to switch topics. The mention of Whitney's name always caused indigestion to swell in his gut. "We're taking an early morning hot air balloon ride—check out the fields. There's still time to sign up if you're interested."

"Just might. Never done a hot air balloon ride before. Could be fun."

The conference started and there was little time for more talk. Jordan attempted to concentrate on the speakers. Megan's presence, so close to him, however, was hard to ignore. He was relieved that they wouldn't be spending the night in the same suite this time. However, the walk back to their connecting rooms later did little to dispel his wandering emotions.

"So, did you and your father find out anything about your brother?" Megan asked as the elevator doors swished shut and the two of them were finally alone.

"No. The police and inspectors are working on it. Dad and I are going to check around town tomorrow when we meet with growers in the field or at the markets. Someone must have seen something."

"It must be hard on both of you, not knowing where he is—if he's okay."

"We have to think positive—if he wasn't in the canal with Gabe, then we must assume he's okay. We'll find him."

"I overheard you talking to Greg about Whitney. If it's any consolation, I agree with you. I wouldn't put it past her to be the one spreading the rumors, causing trouble in order to gain the contract."

"We need to be cautious where she is concerned. Like I said earlier, I'm trying my best not to upset her, while still keeping my distance."

The elevator stopped and the door swished open. Jordan waited for Megan to step from the conveyance and followed her toward their rooms. He stopped alongside her as she inserted the key-card to unlock her door.

"Be sure to order a wake-up call. We leave early. They'll have a breakfast box for us on the bus. In the meantime, if you need anything, just knock. I'm right next door."

"Thanks, Jordan. I'll be fine. I'll see you on the bus."

"Knock on the connecting door tomorrow morning when you're ready. I'll wait for you in the hall. We'll go down together."

The way things had been going, he wanted to make sure she had protection. And if it meant following her every footstep, he was going to be the one to be there for her.

****

The basket tethered to the hot air balloon was larger than Megan had anticipated. Up close, it resembled a giant picnic basket divided into twenty sections big enough to hold two to three people in each sector, depending on their size. Climbing into the contraption was awkward. Thankfully, Megan had worn lightweight slacks and hiking shoes, making it easier to grasp the handles on the outside of the basket, and the strategically placed footholds to climb up the steep side. Sliding over the thick wicker walls was nothing more than cumbersome. Hitching her right leg over the edge, she lost her footing. The depth of the inside pocket deeper than her short legs, her body slammed into the back of the inside pocket. The narrow walls kept her from falling and becoming wedged on the floor. Jordan leaned over the edge, hands gripping the frame of the basket, his eyebrows raised as if she was the clumsiest woman in the entire world.

"Are you okay? You should have waited and let me go first. I would have helped you over."

"A bit late for that now. But yes, I'm okay. I didn't realize how deep these compartments are—they resemble a honeycomb." The top of the basket came to her armpits. She swung her arms over the side and clung to the corded roped edges until her legs stopped shaking. Jordan, on the other hand, practically jumped over and landed next to her in one swift smooth leap. No surprise, really. With his well-toned physique, he probably could jump tall buildings with a single bound.

Megan moved aside in order to accommodate his seductive bulk. Her body temperature rose, her heart thumped, she gazed out over the field and initiated a few breathing exercises to still her inner nerves that at this point had nothing to do with her fear of heights or floating over the Nile with nothing more than a fire induced hot air balloon lifting them and keeping them in the air.

"Relax. It's perfectly safe," Jordan said. "You'll be amazed at how quiet and peaceful it is once we lift off. You'll be floating on thin air."

Good heavens, how would she survive being enclosed in a two by two compartment where every inch of the left side of her body was supported by every inch of the right side of his? Good Lord, they hadn't even left the ground and she was so light-headed there was no way she was going to be able to concentrate on the task ahead. Which was...? Oh, yes—observing farming practices along the Nile far below.

A strong hot puff of heat hissed in the center of the basket as flames shot up into the monstrous balloon. Heat hit Megan's backside. She jumped and clung to Jordan's arm, mouth open, as fire continued to spit upward. The men on the ground released the tethered ropes. The balloon and basket full of people shifted and then ascended into the early morning mist. Jordan's arm circled her shoulders and then slid to her waist. He tugged her against his hot, sexy body. A massive shudder rippled through to her core, and despite her better judgment she leaned against him, her head resting on his chest.

"Are you okay?"

"I'm not sure."

She breathed in his scent—minty breath, fresh morning air, and musk. She was floating on cloud nine—for real—flying on a magic carpet. The hot air balloon slowly drifted high above the ground as if they were standing still.

Holy cow, did he just nuzzle the top of her head? It was getting to be a habit. One she was beginning to enjoy.

It wasn't a good idea to start falling for his charms all over again, even though she felt safe, secure, and…. *Loved*? Taking another moment to soak up the pleasure of being held in his arms, she let a deep sigh escape, placed her hands on his strong chest, and pushed away from his magnetic allure. His arms slowly dropped to his sides, and the early morning air stirred cool between their heated bodies. Megan swung around, clutched the side of the basket, and gazed out over the lush Nile River Basin, surprised to find she was no longer worried about heights as they floated high over the ground. The breathtaking panoramic view was just as seductive as being held in Jordan Kaine's arms. Or standing next to him, where he was now leaning over and looking at the scenery as well. The silence was close to deafening. It had all the trappings of a real live magic carpet ride with a handsome prince. Talk about a time warp.

The bright orange sun rose behind a tall, imposing minaret in the distance, the mist lifting as it washed upward and flowed along with the Nile toward the other side of the valley. Megan looked down into the roofless kitchens, the hot, arid climate and lack of air conditioning forced women to cook in the open for better ventilation. Young children kicked balls, helped in the fields, or lent a hand in the houses below. The fields were spread out in various stages of harvest—all being worked by hand. Donkeys were led along paths to verdant wheat fields. A few of the animals were hitched to wooden wagons that had seen better days. Wheat was harvested and shafted by hand and then piled in the middle of the field. The long, hand-dug canals brought water from the Nile to irrigate the land stretching inland for miles. The lush green banks of the Nile lay in contrast to the desert landscape to the East. Not a single tractor dotted the fields below. Megan turned her camera on video and panned the area.

"Look to your right." Jordan pointed to the rocky, sandy hillside to the east of the basin. "That's the Valley of the Kings. And beyond, over there, is the Valley of the Queens. They've recently found some interesting artifacts in King Tut's tomb."

"There was something about that on the news, but I didn't have a chance to follow up on it." Megan snapped a few pictures of the hillside.

"We should have some free time this afternoon to explore. My father offered to take us through a couple of the burial sites, if you'd like to join us."

"I'd like that, thanks." It hadn't taken her long to become infatuated with Egypt and all the ancient monuments, hieroglyphics, temples, museums, and pyramids. This working project was turning out to be more of an adventure than she'd anticipated. Visiting a dig hadn't even entered her mind yesterday when she'd learned she was to accompany Jordan to his father's excavation site.

They continued to drift high above the Nile. As they turned inland, Jordan pointed to two statues in the middle of an open field.

"The Mennon Statues. They're twin statues of King Amenhotep the third. There was a temple there at one time. These twin statues stood in front of it. It's hard to believe from looking at them from up here that they stand about fifty-nine feet high."

"What happened to the temple?"

"Earthquake. The interesting lore about these statues is that every morning at sunrise there is a sound that surrounds the statues. Some say it is a sad, harmonious song of sorts and now they are referred to as the Singing Stones. There is much more to the legend."

"I'd love to hear it."

"My father can tell the tale much better than I. I'm certain he'll be happy to impart his knowledge. All you have to do is ask."

Megan smiled. With Jordan's Egyptian knowledge, it was surprising he hadn't followed in his father's footsteps.

They were well past the statues when an object was spotted hovering over the Valley of the Kings. The balloon drifted toward their landing site when the object picked up speed and headed their way.

"Look! A drone," one of the passengers shouted.

"More than likely they're taking pictures of the area," Jorden said. "Salah mentioned a slide presentation at tomorrow morning's wind down meeting before we fly back to Cairo."

The drone drew closer. People in the basket smiled and waved, thinking they were being filmed. The contraption made a sharp turn then suddenly zoomed toward them at a reckless speed as if they were its target. In their excitement, everyone started waving and smiling more excitedly when they spotted the camera attached to the front of the drone. Then without warning, the drone flew directly into the ropes connecting the balloon to the basket. The jarring sent the passengers tumbling sideways in shock as the basket tilted. Megan fell against Jordan. His arms circled her protectively, catching her before she fell to her knees, or over the edge.

"What the hell!" Jordan exclaimed as he took in the situation. The mid-sized drone's spinnerets were tangled in the ropes, cutting through at a frenzied pace, and tore through several of the lines. The basket rocked, and then tilted again. The man at the controls quickly reduced the amount of flames shooting upward into the balloon and the basket took an immediate dive. Several of the ropes caught fire.

Two of the passengers on the opposite side of the basket clung precariously to the edge. *Holy Mary, Mother of God.* They were about to plummet to their deaths. The burning ropes were thrown over the side of the basket as they rapidly descended. Passengers screamed and hung on tight.

"Hang on," Jordan ordered. "Sit on my lap and tuck your head against my chest. Keep your arms and legs bent."

Megan didn't question him. If there was half a chance she'd get out of this alive, it would be due to Jordan's level-headedness.

The basket swayed, bobbed, and continued its rapid descent. Passengers were tossed about inside the basket. The couple clinging to the edge of the basket was flung overboard. Their screams echoed throughout the valley. The drone sounded like a buzz saw as it continued to cut through the ropes. Megan closed her eyes and sent up a silent prayer for the couple's safety.

She held her breath and clung to Jordan. She opened her eyes to find another couple clinging to the edge, barely managing to hang on as they drew closer to the ground. One of the men in a nearby pod climbed over his section and grabbed their hands in an effort to keep the couple from falling. The basket rocked as it continued to descend, and their grip loosened. Another man joined in helping the couple, and they were pulled back in to the basket minutes before it hit the ground. Screams filled the air as the balloon lost its buoyancy and drifted over the basket. The basket drifted, dragging along the harvested field as the deflated balloon caught the wind.

Men waiting below rushed to grasp the ropes that were dropped overboard in order to steady the basket. It took several minutes before the basket could be stopped. A mad scramble ensued as passengers jumped overboard before the flaming balloon fully deflated on top of them, and the ropes and material could cause more harm. Getting out wasn't any easier than getting in. Meghan found herself having to bounce on her toes in order to heft her body over the edge. Jordan lifted her up onto the edge, and then quickly jumped seconds before she did. He pivoted and reached for her before they tumbled together on to the wheat field, and solid earth. Stunned, she lay on top of Jordan, her head resting on his chest. His heartbeats thumped in her ear, his arms circled her in a secure hold.

"Are you okay? Are you hurt?" Jordan asked, as he rubbed his hands along her spine, his touch soothing.

"Thanks to you, I'm just winded. You saved my life, Jordan." Being held in his arms had her insides spinning chaotically. If it hadn't been for Jordan, she was certain her body would be bruised, if not broken. But oh, lordy, lying on top of him like this, being held in his warm embrace, did nothing to steady her equilibrium. Nor did the warmth of his lips as he kissed hers before pulling back and loosening his hold.

"Come on then, we need to get away from this contraption before it goes up in flames and sets the field on fire." He shifted her from his body, rolled and stood above her, then grabbed her hands and dragged her to her feet. Hand in hand they raced across the farmer's field until they were a safe distance from the flames. Smoke billowed around the downed balloon. He wrapped her in his arms and held her tight. After the kiss in the basket as they floated high over the Nile, and lying on top of him just now, she was totally out of her element. But, lordy, she felt so safe, cared for, and…, well, it just felt so right to be held in his arms.

"Are you sure you're okay? Are you hurt?"

"Just shaken. Oh, my God, Jordan, what about the others? How did this happen?"

"I don't know. Are you up to giving me a hand to help the others to safety?"

"Of course. Let's do it."

Together they rushed to a woman who lay motionless within a few feet from the burning basket. Without lifting her, they reached under her armpits and dragged the woman a safe distance, then quickly scanned the area for others. Several of those not injured joined in and helped rescue the wounded. The ground crew didn't hesitate once the ropes were secured. They rushed in and helped those needing assistance. A man with a fire extinguisher appeared and before long the fire that had started to spread in the field, as well as the basket, was put out. The pilot, who had been badly burned, was quickly lifted from the basket, placed in a farmer's wagon, and carted off.

The sound of several ambulances in the distance grew louder as they approached. Two police vehicles cut through the field. Officers jumped from their cars, surrounded the drone still attached to the tangled ropes, and left the paramedics to do their job.

The band that had been assigned to welcome everyone back from their flight in traditional musical celebration and dance laid their instruments down and joined in the rescue mission.

Those who weren't whisked away by ambulances, were checked for injuries and taken by wagon to the bus for transport back to town. The ride was quiet, everyone too stunned and in shock to talk. Megan wanted nothing more than to go to her hotel room, take a relaxing, hot sudsy bath, and find a strong cup of coffee. But right now, being held in Jordan's arms was a good place to be. His steady heartbeat as she laid her head on his chest was soothing. She closed her eyes and gave in to the comfort he provided on the bus ride back to town.

Jordan remained by Megan's side as they stepped from the bus and walked into the hotel, his arm securely around her, holding her shaking body. It had been a close call, but they were unharmed.

From the corner of her eye, Megan spotted Whitney having tea at the hotel's outdoor café with one of the conference participants, and two Egyptians from the Ministry of Agriculture. Mr. Delagad was in the process of joining them. She wondered what Whitney was up to now. Even though Whitney had every right to talk to members of the Egyptian Ministry, Megan didn't trust her a single inch. And after their conversation at the dig yesterday, Megan hoped Whitney didn't see Jordan escorting her to the hotel, especially with his arm around her—the woman was jealous enough, she didn't need anything more to add to her cauldron and stir things up.

"I want to call my father, let him know what happened. I don't think this was an accident," Jordan said as they entered the reception area through the glass swinging doors. "And I want to find out if he's heard anything from Caleb. Give me a few minutes and we'll have tea around the corner at the small café where my father and I met yesterday."

"I could use a break to freshen up."

They entered the hotel security entrance station. Megan waited for Jordan to pass through inspection, followed behind, and then the two of them made their way to the elevators, along with a few of the others.

"I'm sorry, Megan," Jordan apologized. "Things certainly haven't gone smoothly since we arrived. Not a good start for a first international travel experience."

Megan agreed, but kept it to herself. If she didn't know any better, she'd swear someone had put a hex on her.

They entered the elevator, along with others returning from the morning fracas. Again, no one spoke, wanting only to get to their rooms and recuperate. When they reached the door to their rooms, Jordan waited while Megan inserted her key card.

"Knock on the door when you're ready," Jordan said. "Take your time."

Jordan entered his own room wondering what the hell he'd been thinking. He had no business kissing Megan, even though it was a reflex reaction heightened by their near death situation. But damn, her skin, silky-smooth, and that pixie auburn hair smelling of whatever the hell sexy shampoo she used had been driving him crazy. Lord Almighty, with her hands wrapped around him, laying on top of him after they'd crashed to the ground earlier, it had invoked feelings that he'd kept at bay since he'd walked into her office and realized who she was—and that he'd be traipsing all over Egypt with her by his side. Thank God she hadn't been seriously injured. She'd be lucky if she wasn't bruised by morning. He had a few aches and pains of his own, some of which had nothing to do with their plummet from the basket. Hell, he had a job to do, dammit. And that didn't involve having an affair with Megan Holloway—although the idea was enticing. Nope. He had no business kissing her.

He had to get his mind back on track. *Fast!*

****

An hour later, Megan sat next to Jordan at the small café down the street from the hotel. Henry Kaine joined them and shared information he'd learned in regards to the search for Caleb.

"I've had word that Caleb has been located," Jordan's father informed them. "A family living on an island who owns a banana farm about ten miles from town is taking care of him."

"Is he all right? Is he hurt?" Jordan asked.

"I talked to Salah. He said Caleb might have a broken arm and leg. Because of the attempt on his life, they didn't think it safe to bring him in just yet."

"So this was more than an accident? They were intentionally attacked. What the hell is going on, Dad?"

"Beats me, son. But Salah is arranging to take me to this island to get Caleb. Find out what he knows."

"When are you going? I want to go, too."

"We're leaving in about an hour. I understand your conference has scheduled an event this afternoon. Won't you need to attend?"

"Megan and Greg can attend and fill me in later. I'm going with you." Jordan turned to Megan, his coffee ignored. "You don't mind working with Greg until I get back, do you?"

"Of course not. I'm here to work."

"He'll make it up to you, Ms. Holloway," Henry Kaine stated. "Jordan can take you for a carriage ride around Luxor—see the temples, especially at night. It's the least he can do."

"He doesn't have to entertain me. I'm not here to play tourist."

"There is much to see while you are here and have the time. Going by carriage to see Luxor temple—especially at night when it is lit, as well as getting a close-up look at Karnak—it is an ideal way to take in all these ancient sites. Besides, Jordan needs to relax, too. So, it is all set."

"Dad…"

"Son, you work too hard. Like I said, you need to relax, too. Besides, I will need to get back to my own work. I apologize, Miss Holloway, as I won't be able to give you that tour of the Valley of the Kings as promised."

"Do not apologize. I've been fortunate to visit several wonderful sites since I arrived in Egypt, thanks to your son sharing his knowledge of Egyptian history. I hadn't anticipated such opportunities when I prepared for the conference, and what I have seen and experienced so far will last a life time."

"This is Megan's first international travel, Dad. I'm sure everything has been overwhelming so far due to all the drama that's been taking place. Perhaps when the conference is over we can extend for a few more days and you can show her around."

"Perfect! Once we get things at the dig straightened out, and bring Caleb back, I'll work up an itinerary for the two of you. I'll give you a tour of the major sites myself."

"That sounds wonderful, Mr. Kaine, but I'm afraid I have other responsibilities at home and won't be able to extend."

"Megan's mother is in a rehab facility. Megan is responsible for her welfare."

"I'm sorry, my dear. Perhaps another time."

"We'll see." Megan smiled at Jordan's father, his offer so appreciated, even though she wouldn't be able to take him up on it. And after talking to her mother's nurse while Jordan was making arrangements with his father earlier, she was certain there was no way she'd be able to extend. Her mother's condition had taken a slight turn. Megan was on pins and needles hoping that things would remain stable until she could return home in a few more days.

Chapter Ten

Jordan handed Megan up into the open horse-drawn carriage, then joined her in the black leather bench seat. He draped his arm along the back edge, circling her neck, his frame filling the tight space between them. There was no inching away from his sexy body even if she wanted to—space didn't allow. She recalled not just one, but two kisses Jordan had bestowed on her in a matter of days. Kisses that had meant to comfort. She was sure he had no idea that his lips lingering on her skin had sent a current of desire radiating straight to her inner core. She was growing too fond of him. Which she shouldn't.

Megan's heartbeat kicked up a notch as the carriage driver nodded in their direction, indicating he was ready to get the tour underway. He turned around and nudged the horse forward. The sound of the horse's hooves hitting the pavement as they clomped down the street brought a smile to Megan's face. She was about to take in the sites of Luxor—sitting next to the sexy Jordan Kaine.

Jordan leaned back, crossed his legs, and sighed. "How are you feeling? Are you sore from our fall? Did you manage to get some rest after this afternoon's session?"

"Yes, thanks. The session finished early, so I returned to my room and had a cup of tea and relaxed. I have a few bruises on my arm, but that's all. We were lucky, Jordan. I was lucky you protected me when I landed on top of you. How are you doing?"

"Bruised ego. Other than that, I'm beginning to think this whole trip is jinxed. Think you'll ever consider another hot air balloon ride?"

"Nope." Megan didn't hesitate. "That was my one and only hot air balloon adventure. I admit I was really enjoying it until the drone attacked. I hope the couple that fell out of the basket survived."

"I heard they were banged up pretty bad. One suffered a few broken ribs and the other had both legs broken, but they'll be okay. The balloon captain was seriously burned. He's going to require a lot of attention and time to recuperate. Others were taken to the hospital and released with minor injuries. Several chose to return to the States to recuperate or get further medical treatment."

"I don't blame them. I'm glad no one was killed. Like you said, this whole trip is turning out to be jinxed."

Jordan breathed in a deep sigh, looked toward the driver, and then faced Megan. "We found Caleb."

"Oh, Jordan, that's wonderful." Megan twisted in her seat and smiled up at him. "Was he badly hurt?"

"A bit banged up—a broken arm and leg. The family who took care of him had him pretty well bandaged, but Dad and I took him to the hospital here in Luxor. Dad is making arrangements to have him flown home, but the authorities won't release him yet."

"Did he have any idea who did this? And why?"

"Caleb didn't want to talk in front of the family that was caring for him. He didn't want to put them in harm's way in case whoever attacked him found out. But he did say something about a smuggling ring and that someone within Dad's group is behind it. He wouldn't say more. The police are going to talk to him later tonight. They have him under protective custody."

"What about your father? Is he in danger?"

"That remains to be seen. I certainly hope not."

"How did Mr. Delagad know where to find your brother?"

"Sixty-four-thousand dollar question. He didn't say. Hopefully Caleb will be able to shed some light on this, or at least enough to help the authorities move in the right direction."

"So what is their next move?"

"Another good question. One I don't have an answer for either, but wish I did. How was this afternoon's session? Were you and Greg able to find out anything we didn't already know in regards to the contract?"

"Not really, mostly a repeat and summary of everything so far. They've rescheduled our field trips for first thing tomorrow morning." Megan wasn't about to tell Jordan about her clash with Whitney. There was trouble enough brewing without Whitney causing more and hampering Jordan's chances of winning the contract and tenure. But if she knew Whitney, if there was a way to do so, she'd give it a try. She'd been working hard at seducing Jordan since their first night in Cairo.

Jordan had enough on his mind. And as far as worrying about Whitney? Well, the best thing for Megan to do was to ignore the snide implications Whitney had thrown in her face. Walking away with

Whitney snickering behind her back hadn't been easy. But Megan had held her head high and had done just that. She had neither confirmed nor denied Whitney's accusations that she was in love with Jordan—nothing would come of it, anyway. Jordan wouldn't act on them and ruin the chance of obtaining tenure.

The carriage slowly meandered down the main thoroughfare along the Nile. The evening sun faded, the cooling temperature soothing. Megan sighed as she gave in to the ambiance of her surroundings.

"Let's just try to relax and take in the sights," Jordan said, his breath tickling the tendrils around her ear. "Let's not even think about the conference." He turned and pointed to his right. "As you can see, Luxor Temple—the Temple of *Amun Ra* –is now to our right. Hard to miss, isn't it?"

"It's huge," she breathed in wonder, awed at the notion of experiencing so much of Egypt's historic past in so few days.

"It is rather awesome. By the time the carriage circles around from our tour, it will be darker and the temple will be lit for the evening. We can get out and stroll around, then walk back to the hotel if you're up to it."

"I am if you are." It sounded romantic. She sighed as the horse continued to clomp along the Corniche Nile Street, passing the Winter Palace Hotel—a British Colonial structure—and several other hotels. When they turned onto Karnak Street, they passed a lively bazaar.

"If we have time, I'd love to visit the bazaar." Megan was captivated by the colorful scarves, dresses, and wraps hanging in the open stalls. There were many trinkets, touristy items, and various spicy aromas that filled the evening air.

"I'm sure we can arrange it," Jordan said, taking her hand in his. "But it would have to be a short stop after our field trips tomorrow."

A warm tingly sensation shot to her heart as he softly rubbed his thumb over the palm of her hand. Did he know what his touch was doing to her?

"What about tonight? It really isn't far from our hotel." She attempted to withdraw her hand from his, but his hold was steady—firm.

"Sure. We can stop at the hotel first. I've arranged to meet Greg tonight to see what else he's found out. Then we can wander over and check it out."

She was already under the spell of Egypt, and riding in a horse-drawn carriage with Jordan Kaine by her side, caressing her hand as if they were lovers, had her imagination soaring, and her insides humming. It didn't help her resolve any when his arm drew more snug around her shoulders and his fingers gently caressed her bare arm. A current of desire rippled through to her chest and lingered. The urge to inch closer and be held tightly against him had her senses reeling. Ahhh, what would it be like to experience a real kiss before the night drew to a close? She gazed at the bustling streets, the many carriages, the colorful hodge-podge, the scents, and the many sounds as it all swirled around her as if she was in a fairytale come to life.

The carriage continued on for several more minutes as she took it all in. And then she spotted one of Luxor's famous statue groupings.

"Oh, look, it's the human-headed Sphinxes," Megan exclaimed, sitting up to get a better view of the long row of ancient Sphinxes, successfully disengaging from Jordan's magnetic hold. His hand slipped from her arm, his grip from her hand loosened.

"Impressive, isn't it?" Jordan said, straightening in the seat and reverting back to history guide mode. "In ancient times the avenue linked the Temple of Luxor to the Temple of Karnack. It was a long processional avenue leading from one to the other."

The carriage passed over the Avenue, and then circled around the Temple of Luxor, giving them a much closer look, and a breathing space Megan so desperately needed. The driver slowed the carriage, smiled, and pointed to the entrance.

"The entrance. Two statues of Ramesses II," the driver said in his broken English. "Built by Amenhotep III in the fourteenth century. Ramesses II himself finished it. You will see later when they put on the lights."

The visual was too much for Megan to digest in so short a time. The driver turned back to his horse, and the carriage continued along the busy streets. The clear azure sky began to fade as the sun descended for the evening. The hot, dry temperatures dropped to a comfortable degree. Megan relaxed. Her head nodded sideways. She caught herself before it landed on Jordan's shoulder.

"You're tired. Go ahead and rest your head on my shoulder. There isn't much else to see right now. We'll be back at the temple in about ten minutes."

"Sorry. I'll be okay. Like you said, it's been a trying few days. I guess it's all catching up to me."

"No need to apologize. Come here and rest your head."

Before she had a chance to resist, he wrapped her in his arm and drew her against his body once again. He nuzzled the top of her head. She bolted up out of his arms.

"What?" The confusion on Jordan's face was comical.

"You've got to stop doing that."

"What? What'd I do?"

"You know what you did. Kissing me on top of my head. This is not a romantic holiday, Jordan—its work. I don't want to do anything to ruin our chances of winning this contract, or you getting tenure. Isn't it bad enough Whitney showed up, and has caught you kissing me? She is one jealous lady. And unless I miss my guess, she's out for revenge."

"It's none of Whitney's business who I kiss."

"I agree, but-."

"Shut up and let me kiss you properly."

Before she had a chance to think about what he intended, his lips were on hers in a deep, mind-blowing kiss filled with promises that he shouldn't be offering— or her accepting. Nevertheless, her insides spun out of control and she found herself leaning in to the kiss. And wanting more. Much more.

Her arms wound around his neck. She gave in to the need coursing through her body. Holy Hanna, the man could kiss. And just as quickly as he started the kiss, it ended. He put his strong hands on her arms and separated her from him as much as the space in the carriage would allow.

"I've wanted to do that ever since you walked toward me at the Ithaca airport."

Speechless. She was totally without words. They gazed into each other's eyes. She could see the desire in his and wondered what he saw in hers. Because right now she really wanted him to kiss her again. But there was no way she should let it happen. He should never have kissed her with such abandon in the first place. But oh, lordy, she wanted another one of his kisses. Now!

"You took my breath away," he continued. "Watching you walk down the terminal with that pixie haircut. You looked so lovely, so lost. I wanted to take you in my arms right then and there."

"Jordan-"

"Let me finish. I was as stunned as you when we shared a suite in Cairo. God, Megan, you have no idea what ideas filled my brain when I saw the astonished expression on your lovely face. You were as overwhelmed as I was with the accommodations. I had a hard time keeping my hands to myself, not storming your room and…, well, it's been hard keeping my feelings to myself. This whole trip has been frustrating, to say the least. But then Whitney showed up and all the old fiasco with her sexual harassment charges…, well, it stopped me in my tracks. I didn't want you to think I was that pervert about to take advantage of you. But this morning's accident really shook me up. When you landed in my arms, it was like a wake-up call. With you lying on top of me, well, it was like I'd found my favorite glove—the fit was perfect. God, if something had happened to you and I missed my chance, I don't know what I would have done."

"Jordan. Please. To begin with, it was a wonderful kiss. And I've never thought of you as a pervert. We all knew what Whitney was like, thinking she could ace your class. She used you."

"Thank you for that. Others weren't as understanding."

"Is that what happened? Why you aren't married now? I remember you were engaged. Did Whitney cause a break up?"

"On a dime. Luckily we weren't married."

"I'm sorry. It must have been hard for you."

"More than I can say. But the worst part was dealing with teaching a class filled with females who gave me those looks—either they'd heard the rumors and shied away from me, which was okay, or those who thought they could take advantage of my sexual prowess—that I didn't and don't possess, by the way. I took a short leave of absence until things blew over."

"I never said or did anything to let on, but I sort of had a crush on you back then, too. But there was no way I was going to act on my emotions. I understood you were engaged. And then Whitney happened."

He drew her to him, wrapped his arms around her, and kissed her until her toes curled.

The carriage stopped in front of Luxor Temple, now lit for the evening. The driver's smile, as he cleared his throat, caused Megan's checks to burn.

"We'll finish this later," Jordan beamed, and then assisted her from the carriage. He paid the driver, and hand in hand they entered the ancient Temple of *Amun-Ra*.

Megan's heart burst with happiness. Lindsey's words echoed in her head. Had Jordan just intimated what she thought he had? Was she ready to accept his unspoken invitation?

Jordan's hand tightened in hers as he lead her through the temple entrance and the tall pillars festooned with hieroglyphics, topped with open lotus blossoms that reached toward the heavens. It was all too much to take in, but the ambiance, with Jordan by her side, made the evening come alive with ancient vibes. They walked through the many different architectural columns, some rounded with open papyrus capitals reaching to the heavens, and some bundled with capped tops. They passed groups of statues representing both gods and pharaohs. Jordan, thanks to his father's teachings, highlighted several of the objects, including the obelisk and façade of the temple.

Later, leaving the temple hand in hand, they strolled along the Avenue of the Sphinxes in the evening light, and then turned left toward the spice market. Megan caught the scent of the market a block before they entered the long street where stalls of a myriad of spices were arranged in large bowls, some in deep wicker baskets, and some hanging from wires. Farther in, they strolled past stalls selling clothing, shoes, assorted household items, and souvenirs.

"Is that an Aladdin's lamp?" Megan stopped, smiling as she pointed to a shelf lined with various shapes of tea pots resembling the elongated magic genie lamps from the movie. "I bet a young girl would love to have one of those to rub and make a wish."

Before Megan contemplated his intentions, Jordan purchased the lamp while she was looking at the colorful spices in a connecting stall. He presented it to her, arms outstretched, dimples smiling, and his eyes bright with a touch of humor.

"Jordan! You didn't have to buy that for me."

"I couldn't resist. Remember, you only get three wishes."

Megan couldn't hide her own smile as she accepted the gift. If genie wishes really did come true, then she had an urgent situation needing help—the wish that her mother's health would improve so that she would be able to come home from the facility and resume a normal life once again. Megan would have to think hard about the other two wishes. But with Jordan's hot kiss earlier, and the warm, sensual emotions emanating from him all evening, she didn't think she'd have to waste a wish to ask for an evening of bliss being held in his arms—all night long.

"Aren't you going to rub the lamp and make a wish?" His saucy smile made her insides squirm with pleasure.

"I think I'll wait a while. Make sure it's something I really desire and can't live without."

"Good thinking. If you need any help, let me know." He leaned over and captured her lips. She clung to the lamp nestled between them. He lifted his head and gave her a suggestive smile, his eyes deep pools of desire.

"I think it's time to head back to our rooms."

Megan didn't argue.

Chapter Eleven

In her wildest dreams she'd never anticipated making love to Jordan Kaine. Well, maybe back in her college years, and for a second when her friend Lindsey might have planted that suggestion in her brain before she left for Egypt. But nothing—definitely nothing—had prepared her for last night. His lovemaking far exceeded her expectations. Caving in to his charms, his seductive mouth, hands, and his touch had her melting in his arms. They'd hardly made it inside his hotel room when he'd kissed her like there really was no tomorrow. By the time they'd made it across the floor toward his bedroom, both their clothes lay scattered on the floor. She'd had a hard time finding everything on her way to her own room later, after Jordan had fallen asleep. She hadn't wanted to leave his side. But darn those second thoughts—the possible repercussion of her actions and having to face him in the morning—had washed over her. Still, her body ached for more of Jordan Kaine.

After lying in her own bed where sleep eluded her for the next two hours, Megan finally hit the shower, dressed, and prepared her bag to carry on the bus for their morning field trips—note pad, camera, motion sickness tablets, comb, sunscreen, mini binoculars, IPad, water bottle, and breath mints. She dressed in loose, lightweight black slacks, an aqua tank top, and her standard white gauzy long-sleeved blouse. Her favorite blue lapis earrings, simple Timex watch, and sand-sturdy shoes completed the outfit. She placed her Indiana Jones-type hat next to her bag, and settled on the sofa, her head resting on the overstuffed decorated Egyptian pillow. The sleep that had eluded her earlier, dragged her under, dreams of making love to Jordan wrapped around her like a warm blanket. Megan shut her eyes to savor the magic of the night—and to savor the sensual emotions still humming deep inside—and fell fast asleep.

****

Jordan woke to find Megan gone from his bed. She'd gone back to her room sometime during the night. Oh, God, did she regret their lovemaking already? He rolled over and stared at the ceiling. What the hell had he done leading Megan on like that? Seducing her while riding in the carriage, not to mention making love to her last night, especially with the contracts and tenure so important. Not a smart move, Kaine. Shit. Tenure be dammed! Megan Holloway was every bit the sensual lover he'd envisioned her to be. A sexy pixie—a pleasurable surprise for sure. His heart had been fully engaged. He thought hers had too.

He jumped out of bed, hauled on his pants, and headed for their connecting door. He knocked several times. No answer. Damn! Hopefully she wasn't ignoring him and was in the shower getting ready for the day. He headed for his shower, a smile on his face as his thoughts returned to their night of shared sex. Hell, it was more than sex, it was the best lovemaking he'd ever had—his heart and soul was fully involved. He couldn't wait to see her this morning, take her in his arms and show her how serious he was about what they had shared last night—twice, at least. He'd lost count. He'd give her fifteen more minutes and knock on her door again so they could go down to breakfast together.

Fifteen minutes later there was still no answer on the connecting door. With a sigh, Jordan grabbed his gear and headed down to the breakfast buffet to look for her. They needed to talk. He didn't want her to think what they'd shared was a one-night stand. He wanted more. Much more.

Happier than he'd been in a long time, he entered the restaurant, a smile on his face.

He spotted Megan sitting with Ruth and Harold, and several others from the conference. She spotted him and dropped her head as if her plate full of food was the most important thing in the world, her cheeks flushed. But Jordan caught the desire, longing, and was that a touch of sadness in her gorgeous eyes? Hopefully the glitter was of excitement, not tears.

He headed her way but was pulled up short when a hand latched on to his arm and drew him around to meet none other than Whitney Nash. Dammit. Just what he didn't need this morning. From the smug look on her face, Whitney had seen the meaningful exchange between him and Megan just now. Double damn. He didn't want to talk to Whitney regardless of whether or not it had anything to do with the conference. He yanked his arm from her hand and stepped back. He caught the shock and disappointment on Whitney's face before she morphed into a smiling, sexy predator.

"I see you're up to your old tricks, Jordan." Whitney actually cooed. "I'm sure it's not going to help you get tenure anytime soon."

"As long as you don't go stirring things up again, I'm positive it won't. Don't you think you've done enough damage already? If I were you I'd mind your own business and concentrate on the conference and your own contract proposal. I've been patient in not aggressively spurning your advances, but you don't seem to be able to get the message. So let me tell it to you straight. I am not interested in you—never have been. So stop interfering in my personal life. You've done enough damage as it is. Grow up and concentrate on cleaning up your own act instead of ruining others' lives. You'll be a much happier person."

Jordan didn't wait for her response. Instead, he turned and, no longer hungry, headed toward the coffee station. He needed a strong cup of Joe to help calm down and figure out what he was going to do next. He'd just pissed off Whitney—no telling what she would do to retaliate. He'd have to be more alert now than before. And Megan? How could he discuss such a personal matter with her, about them, in a room full of people? Assure her that last night wasn't a mistake—and that he'd finally told Whitney to take a hike regardless of the consequences.

Jordan poured a large mug of coffee, grabbed a pastry filled with fruit, and scanned the room for a seat. He spotted Greg at a table with Salah Delagad, and another man he didn't know, and headed their way.

"Good morning, gentlemen. May I join you?" Jordan asked.

"Please, have a seat." Greg indicated an empty chair.

Jordan placed his coffee and pastry on the round table top and joined the men.

"Jordan, I don't believe you've met Dr. Norland from Florida," Greg introduced the tall, tanned man who looked to be in his forties.

Jordan extended his arm across the table and shook the man's hand. "Pleasure to meet you. I don't believe I've seen you around."

"Arrived late last night—messed up flight arrangements."

"Sorry to hear that," Jordan said.

"At least you missed the hot air balloon incident," Greg stated. "I wasn't involved, but Jordan and a few others were. Thankfully, no one was killed. A couple was badly injured. They are still in the hospital. Others sustained mostly bumps and bruises."

"I checked on them this morning," Salah informed them. "They are improving. It is unfortunate that several will not be able to continue with the program."

"I'm sorry to hear that." Dr. Norland placed his coffee cup in its saucer and sat back in his chair. "So, what's today's schedule?"

"The conference organizers have made provision for an additional field visit this morning. You will not be disappointed." Greg smiled at the group sitting around the table.

"Buses should be outside in an hour," Salah informed the men. "I have arranged for everyone to visit a village on an island where they grow bananas and oranges."

"Greg's specialty," Jordan said. "Should be an interesting morning."

This was the island where they had found Caleb. Had Salah made the special arrangements while they were there to find his brother? Or was that how he'd learned of Caleb's whereabouts? He didn't want to ask Salah in front of the others, but there were still a lot of unanswered questions in regards to the incidents that had been taking place. Salah seemed to know more than he was letting on.

Jordan wanted to ask him if the family was still under surveillance, but now wasn't the time. He didn't want to involve the others in his father's affairs. In fact, he needed to talk to his father, again. See if the police had unearthed any clues in regards to the accidents that had been happening at the site. And determine whether there was a connection to the balloon incident. Somehow it had the makings of an intentional assault on the conference attendees. But why? They had nothing to do with his father's dig.

General conversation continued as Jordan finished his coffee. He kept his eye on Megan the entire time, but she didn't look his way. He finally excused himself to go to his room and retrieve his gear for the day, and to meet with Megan so they could talk about last night. He looked across the cafeteria to where Megan was sitting only to find she had vanished. He made a mad dash for his room, wanting to catch her before they got on the bus.

But he was too late. Or she wasn't answering her door—again.

Dammit. She *was* ignoring him.

****

Instead of going back to her room, Megan had brought her day bag with her in anticipation of avoiding Jordan. She wasn't quite ready to face him this morning. Instead, she used the restaurant facilities, and then headed for the buses waiting in front of the hotel.

Already people were boarding. She joined them, and headed toward the back of the bus, hoping it would fill up around her, and Jordan would have to sit somewhere else. Unfortunately, that didn't happen.

"Why are you avoiding me?" Jordan asked as he swung in to the seat and sat next to her—closer than Megan considered necessary.

Megan inched closer to the window. "I'm not."

"Yes, you are. After last night," he whispered in her ear, "I would have thought that was impossible."

His breath against her skin was a soft caress, evoking memories of what they had shared last night. She stood her ground—her head high, her shoulders straight. She faced him. A mistake. She saw the longing, the concern, and the hurt in his eyes. She almost caved.

She cleared her throat. Despite knowing how Jordan really felt about Whitney, Megan couldn't help lashing out. "After last night I wouldn't have thought you'd be flirting so openly with Whitney Nash this morning—of all people."

His eyes grew dark as he met hers—stare for stare. His words were cool, but precise. "I wasn't flirting with Whitney, and you know it. You know how I feel about her, and after last night, how I feel about you. If you'd really been paying attention earlier you'd know I told her to get lost. I'm sure she was throwing daggers at my back as I walked away—looking for you."

The two of them continued to stare at each other, Megan wanting to squirm, but held still—until he broke the silence.

"Why did you run away in the middle of the night? God, Meg, I missed you…"

Megan lowered her eyes and panned the passengers sitting close by in an attempt to gauge who might be listening in on their conversation. "Do you really want to have this conversation within hearing distance of everyone on the bus?" she whispered.

He reached over and clasped his hand on top of one of hers and drew it over his knee. His tight hold warmed her insides. She wanted to snuggle against him, feel his body close to hers once again. But she was brought up short by his words, whispered for only their ears.

"You're right. Now isn't the time. But don't think I'm going to let this go. We shared something special last night. I was hoping you felt it too."

He squeezed her hand. She couldn't look at him, and instead turned and gazed out the window— straight into Whitney's knowing glare as she waited to board the second bus. If looks could kill, Megan would be slumped over dead.

On the bus ride along the rich fertile land along the Nile, Megan sat next to the window, camera at the ready. Like before, the fields along the river were impressive, especially as most of the work was done by hand—no large machinery assisted the field hands. Donkeys carted wagons to and from the fields carrying produce and wheat after being shafted by hand in the middle of the fields. Children splashed in the river while women washed clothes. Tall reeds and feathery date palms waved in the breeze along the river banks while gray water buffalo turned wooden waterwheels. And all the while Megan was aware of her feelings for Jordan, and the fact that he didn't leave her side all morning.

An hour later, they moved on to a second field, and then crossed the Nile by small boats to the island and the village that produced bananas and oranges—the island where they had found Caleb.

The heat penetrating, Megan was glad she had worn a lightweight blouse and large-rimed hat. After the tour of the main banana site, they were taken to a pavilion where the women of the village provided light refreshments. Whitney kept to herself during the rest of the field tours, and conversation, except for work related topics, was impossible between Megan and Jordan. Before she knew it, they were back on the bus for their return trip to Luxor. Soon after the bus was underway, they were given box lunches—sandwiches of ham and cheese, hard-boiled eggs, a banana, and orange juice. And once again, intimate conversation was impossible. But the tug of sexual tension burning at her insides convinced her they needed to talk. She needed to know where this relationship was going—if they had a relationship.

She hoped and prayed that they had a relationship.

****

Greg waylaid Jordan when they stepped from the bus. Upset at the delay from being unable to set things straight with Megan all morning, Jordan begrudgingly stepped aside as Megan and the others entered the hotel, and then joined Greg.

"I'd say you've got it bad, my friend." Greg laughed. "I'd be cautious if I were you. You don't want to mess up tenure."

"Don't know what you're talking about." Jordan smiled at his friend, and let Greg lead him to the outdoor café down the street.

"Just watch your step."

"So what's so important that we have to talk? Did you find out anything while we were on the island?"

"Yes, but it's not about Egyptian agriculture. There is rumor that the balloon incident was not an accident. Word is that it was intentional."

"I assumed as much, but to what end? Why is the conference being targeted?"

"Not the conference, per se. You."

"What? Why me?" Joran sat back in his chair, stunned. "What the hell have I done?"

"Actually, the scuttlebutt is that someone has a grudge against your father, thus you and your brother. Seems Henry Kaine and his sons are trying to take over not only the Egyptian digs, but their agriculture."

"Where did you hear this? Who?"

"Apparently Whitney gave Dr. Norland an earful this morning at breakfast."

Jordan's stomach clenched. Whitney! Why was he not surprised? She'd tried to warn him about the rumors. Maybe warn him was too accurate a word as far as Whitney was concerned, but he should have listened more carefully—paid more attention to her instead of brushing her words aside. It was more than a case of obtaining the contract—now, it was a matter of safety. Which meant Megan was also in danger, as were other conference attendees. And all because he was Henry Kaine's son? Which meant, in order to keep Megan safe, he needed to distance himself from what-ever-the-hell he'd started last night. Letting his emotions interfere in their mission here in Egypt wasn't the wisest move he'd ever made. But damn, the passion they'd shared filled him to the brim with wanting more.

His gut clenched. He removed his sunglasses and rubbed his hand over his face. "Shit, Greg, what the hell are we going to do?"

"Good question. As you know, the authorities are investigating the incidents." Greg leaned forward, keeping his voice low. "According to Dr. Norland, they think it has something to do with the smuggling operation that seems to have started up about two months ago. Apparently, they're checking to see if there is a connection with the other digs—see if they can find a common link."

"Have the authorities identified anyone yet? It must be someone my father knows—someone who has access to his research and site. Probably an insider." Jordan rested his elbows on the round table top. Instead of coffee, he needed a drink. Who knew a simple conference could end up being so dangerous.

"They're looking into that." Greg shook his head. "We leave tomorrow evening, but I suspect whatever is going on here in Luxor will follow us to Cairo."

"You could be right. I'm going to check with my father. Maybe we should talk to Salah, as well, see what he knows. After all, he was the one who knew where Caleb was being kept on the island we just visited."

"Speaking of Caleb, was he able to shed any light on who attacked him and Gabe?" Greg asked.

"I talked to Caleb earlier today, but he was close-mouthed about it," Jordan said. "He told me he'd already talked to the authorities and couldn't say much. Didn't want to hamper the investigation in case word got out to the wrong person. He's under strict watch and will remain in the hospital a couple more days. But

I plan to visit my father, make sure he's safe and see how I can help."

Damn. His talk with Megan was going to have to wait—again.

"Do me a favor, Greg, and keep an eye on Megan for me while I go out to the dig. Who knows what this person—or persons—have planned next. What time is our flight to Cairo tomorrow?"

"Six o'clock." Greg grinned knowingly. "I'll keep an eye on Megan for you. I just hope you know what you're doing, man. There is too much riding on our proposal."

"Yes. Yes, there is," Jordan confirmed, his mind racing at the implications of something happening not only to his father, but to Megan as well. If anything happened to her, it would be because of him—a Kaine. He couldn't let that happen. "See if you can get an earlier flight and the two of you get out of Luxor."

Chapter Twelve

"I had warned you, Habib. No one was to be killed," Salah Delagad rasped. "You have gone too far."

"Omar and his men got carried away—as the Americans say, an accident. Collateral damage."

"You are lucky they did not kill Henry Kaine's son, Caleb. Or that his other son Jordan Kaine was not injured in the balloon incident that you orchestrated."

"I tell you, the murder was not my intent." Habib's voice grated angrily. "As for the balloon snafu, no one was killed."

"They could have been killed or more seriously injured. Many of those people are not connected with the Kaines."

"Again, nothing more than collateral damage, should that happen."

Habib needed to be taken down sooner rather than later.

"You have no proof that the Kaines are responsible for the theft of the antiquities that have been uncovered at their excavation site," Salah stated. He leaned across the table, pointing a finger at Habib. "In fact, Jordan Kaine's team made it a point to bring Ms. Holloway from the Wild and Wonderful Corporation to make sure our specific procedures were being followed on their farm visits. From where I stand, the Kaines are innocent of any wrong doing."

"What proof do you have? Are they not from New York?" Habib spat. "Are not the smugglers in cahoots with those in New York City—the Big Apple? Do you not see the connection?"

"If I were you, Habib, I'd look to your right-hand man, Omar. I have heard rumors from the authorities—his name has been mentioned along with a few others on your payroll that have dealings with the New York gang."

"Omar? He is loyal to me. If I find out he is responsible for stealing and helping to smuggle our country's treasures, he will not live long enough to see another day."

"If he is the guilty one, then you need to apologize to the Kaine family and stop your foolish vendetta. You have put them through enough."

"I apologize to no one in an effort to protect what is ours."

"Tread carefully, my friend. I hear Henry Kaine's son Caleb has talked to the authorities while in his hospital bed. They are ready to arrest those who are guilty of causing the researcher's death, as well as cracking down on the smuggling ring." Salah hoped his warning was more than sufficient to cause Habib to force his hand and search out Omar, who had gone missing.

Salah was sorry he had used Ms. Nash to spread lies about Jordan Kaine once he'd learned of her own vendetta against the American Professor and his lady friend Ms. Holloway. Bringing situations such as theirs out in the open often led to one betraying the other. The authorities had kept close watch to double check their facts. He was relieved to learn that although Ms. Nash was a bitter woman, there was no evidence of any of them being connected to the smuggling scheme.

****

Jordan's mind wandered as he drove the small dilapidated open-air jeep along the desert road to his father's dig. He hated to leave Megan's safety in Greg's hands, but he had no choice. The Kaine name had suddenly become a target—Megan would be safer without him by her side. It was a wonder that those involved in the balloon mishap had all survived. If anything had happened to Megan—any of them for that matter—it would have been because of him. He could only imagine how she was coping with the events since becoming part of their team. He had to admit after the first few setbacks on the plane, she'd proven herself the capable, organized, caring person Helen had made her out to be, and he'd wanted to make her first international experience a memorable one. But not to the point that she never wanted to travel again. Especially to Egypt where there was so much more he wanted to show her. Perhaps it was a good thing she hadn't wanted to talk about last night—a night of passion. And one she obviously already regretted.

A wise decision on her part, after all.

Jordan stopped the jeep next to the tent, put it in park, and jumped out. His father met him as he rounded the vehicle.

"Son, what are you doing here? Didn't you say you had meetings tonight and you had to prepare to leave tomorrow?"

"My plans have changed. Greg has things under control with our contracts. I gave him my recommendations. Right now, I'm more concerned for your safety. There are rumors of smuggling connected with your dig—that you are being implicated, as well as Caleb. And, that I'm a possible connection through the conference. The Kaine name has become tarnished."

"But we are not connected with any smuggling ring." His father stared from beneath the brim of his hat, his hands spread out in front of him pleading his case. "I've been adamant from the beginning that any artifacts we uncover stay right here in Egypt."

"Whoever is behind this rumor thinks otherwise. The balloon incident wasn't an accident, Dad. It was intentional. The authorities have requested that I stay in Luxor until the situation is resolved. I would have stayed anyway—make sure we clear our family name. Whether or not I obtain the contract with the Ministry of Agriculture is immaterial to me at this point."

"What about your tenure?"

"Not making tenure doesn't mean I'll lose my job. It just means I won't obtain tenure. I can live with that. What I can't live with is my family—you—coming to harm."

"I love you too, son. Appreciate your support, as I know Caleb does, as well."

As they moved from the front of the vehicle toward the canopy in the middle of the desert, Jordan's chest swelled with pride at his father's sentiments—his family bonds ran deep.

"Let's find a cool drink and sit," his father suggested. "I've been out in this god-forsaken sun too long already today. We can fill each other in on what we already know, see if we can find any links that might be useful."

When they reached the tent, they removed their hats and sun glasses, grabbed a water bottle from the ice chest, and settled in camp chairs.

"So, what's our next move?" Jordan asked "Have you talked to Caleb?"

"Yes. I've talked to him, and the authorities. And I'm confident that none of my crew is involved in stealing artifacts. Can you say the same about those collaborating with you?"

"I've known Greg for years. He's an upstanding colleague."

"What about your Ms. Holloway?"

"Megan? Trust me, she is not involved. She is the most trust-worthy, caring person I know."

And soft, sensual, and loving—oh God, the loving….

"Ms. Nash, then? What about her?"

Jordan's stomach clenched at the mention of her name. "I have no doubt she would try to ruin our chances of obtaining the Egyptian contracts, but somehow I don't think she would go so far as smuggling. I don't think she would do well in prison."

"At this point, then, we must let the authorities follow their leads, and continue to keep our heads above water. Now, if you have time, I'd like to show you our latest finds."

"I'm not going anywhere until this situation has been resolved."

"Well, then, come on. Might as well help an old man out and learn something while you're at it."

Jordan's lopsided grin grew wider as he followed his father out from under the tent into the hot desert sun. It was going to be a long evening.

****

Megan woke from a sleepless night. Jordan was ignoring her. He hadn't answered her knocks on their connecting door last night, or this morning. It only proved one thing. He had gotten the message she had been sending him all day yesterday. But now she was ready to talk. Perhaps she could catch up with him at breakfast. She quickly showered, dressed, packed her bags for their flight back to Cairo, and went in search of Jordan.

Megan scanned the cafeteria. Jordan was nowhere in sight. She sighed, lost her appetite, and instead of getting in line for the buffet, headed straight for the coffee station in the far corner next to the window overlooking the Nile. The pristine, cloudless Persian blue sky was picture-perfect. Felucca sails were spread wide and billowed in the morning breeze as they waited for passengers lining up along the riverbanks to board for a morning adventure on the river. The short ride on the Nile she had shared with Jordan and members of the conference had been ruined by Whitney's accusations. After the night spent in Jordan's arms, she envisioned them sailing down the Nile in one of Egypt's ancient looking felucca style sailboats. Had she ruined her chances of a relationship with Jordan?

Where was her genie lamp when she needed it?

A wishful sigh escaped, her shoulders slumped as she turned, and spotted Greg sitting alone at a table along the far wall. Coffee in hand, Megan made a bee-line for his table. She needed answers.

"Mind if I join you?"

"Not at all. Actually, I have a message for you from Jordan. Are you sure you don't want breakfast first?"

"Thanks, but I'll be fine as soon as I get this coffee down me."

"Sleepless night?"

"Something like that. So what about Jordan?"

Greg directed his gaze at his eggs benedict, fork paused above the plate. He didn't look her in the eye. What was going on?

"Greg?"

"He left a message for me saying he was staying behind. Apparently, the authorities have learned that there might be a connection between the accidents at Jordan's father's dig and the balloon incident. Jordan plans to stay and help his father figure out what is going on."

"Jordan isn't coming back to Cairo with us today?" Megan's voice pitched an octave before she caught herself and lowered it so her voice wouldn't echo across the room. "Is everything okay? What's really going on here, Greg?"

"Apparently there are rumors of smuggling artifacts—a ring connected to New York. Jordan wants us to go on to Cairo and deal with the proposal—make sure nothing is amiss with our contacts. We can present our findings and strategies we want to initiate as scheduled. Jordan gave me his reports. Anything you've managed to come up with, as well as the photographs you've taken, I can incorporate in our report. We can go over it together on the flight to Cairo."

Megan listened to Greg talk about the conference, their proposal, the contracts, but didn't hear a word. Not only was Henry Kaine in danger and being accused of smuggling, but Jordan was being implicated as well. From Greg's demeanor, she was sure there was something more he wasn't telling her? What was so important that Jordan had to stay behind?

"Why does Jordan have to stay in Luxor?"

"Other than trying to help figure out the connection between these incidents, he wants to make sure his father and brother remain safe. Apparently, Caleb finally talked to the authorities and mentioned a few names. Jordan didn't say who, but the authorities are looking into several leads. It could possibly be an insider."

"An insider at both the dig and the conference?" Megan was reminded of Omar Nagid and Salah Delagad—could they be involved? And the man Omar had been talking to in the desert at the dig when Jordan and his father were looking for answers as to Caleb's whereabouts?

"There was a man Dr. Nagid was talking to at the dig when Jordan and I were there. The man disappeared when Jordan and his father joined Dr. Nagid at the crest of the hill. I took a series of pictures that day, perhaps there is one of them. What if I showed them to the authorities? Do you think that might help the case?"

"It couldn't hurt. We have ample time before our flight leaves. Have something to eat, grab your camera, and meet me in the hotel lobby. I'll go with you to the police station and see if they're interested in downloading your photos."

Megan didn't hesitate. If it would help solve the case and help keep Jordan and his family out of harm's way, it was the least she could do.

Greg was waiting next to the lobby exit when Megan returned.

"I've hired a taxi to save time. Are you ready?"

"Yes. But I've been thinking. What about the others? If the balloon incident wasn't an accident, then it put everyone else in danger, too. Are you sure Jordan is being singled out?"

"It crossed Jordan's mind that others were put in danger because of his connection with his father. One of the reasons he's decided to stay behind until they can wrap things up here. If it takes him out of the equation, then there shouldn't be any more accidents involving those attending the conference."

"Still…"

"We'll let the authorities handle it. Our job is to focus on the contracts."

Megan had other thoughts. If Jordan was putting himself in danger to save the others and something happened to him before they had a chance to talk, she'd never forgive herself for purposely side-stepping his attempts for them to work things out.

She was such a coward.

Chapter Thirteen

During the short flight to Cairo, Megan discussed the proposal to be presented to the Ministry of Agriculture with Greg. Her mind, however, kept recalling the danger surrounding Jordan, his father, and brother—at least it took her mind off the flight itself, having forgotten to take any Dramamine. She and Greg had been surprised to find Mr. Delagad meet them when they had arrived at the police station. He'd introduced them to the authorities, who had been very pleasant, although formal, and extremely interested in the disk full of pictures she had taken. They immediately downloaded them into their system. They were, however, not forthcoming with details about the case, and thanked them for their assistance.

Arriving in Cairo later that day, they were once again taken to their hotel by taxi. Megan's trepidation this time had nothing to do with being a novice traveler. Leaving Jordan behind in Luxor—in possible danger—had her heart beating overtime.

Megan wheeled her carryon-bag through security, then to the reception desk to register. After giving her name, she was handed a keycard along with her room number.

"A message arrived for you this morning, madam." The clerk smiled as she handed Megan an envelope. "If there is anything we can do to make your stay a pleasant one, please do not hesitate to inform us. Have a good day."

Megan thanked the receptionist and waited for Greg to finish registering. Hopefully the message was from Jordan and everything was okay. Thinking it a private message, she waited until they rode the elevator to the 11th floor where she and Greg parted to go to their separate rooms.

"Give a knock when you're settled in. We'll have lunch before our meeting this afternoon," Greg said, waiting for her to make sure her keycard worked.

"Give me about forty-five minutes," Megan said, wanting time to read her message, and freshen up after the flight.

"See you then," Greg called over his shoulder as he headed down the hall to find his room.

Megan entered her suite and, ignoring the beautifully appointed Egyptian motifs scattered around the room, she rushed to the sofa, sat, and slid open the envelope, anxious to discover what Jordan had to say. With shaking hands, she slipped the single sheet of paper from the hotel embossed envelope, unfolded it, and gasped. *Oh, No!* It wasn't a note from Jordan at all, but an urgent message from the facility where her mother had been staying. Her mother had had another stroke and was in hospital. Would Megan please come home as soon as possible?

Megan's shaking hands holding the message dropped to her lap. She leaned her head on the back of the sofa and shut her eyes. So much for wishing on the genie lamp. Could her life get any more complicated? This whole trip was a mistake—she should never have agreed to the assignment, regardless of needing a good review. Her mother was right. She could find another job—one that didn't involve traveling to foreign lands.

And falling in love with Jordan Kaine.

First things first. She needed to call Mrs. Wilson—find out her mother's status. Then, she needed to make flight arrangements to fly back home. Hopefully she could schedule a flight out today. She'd call Lindsey and ask her to pick her up at the airport when she arrived home.

She'd done whatever it was she was supposed to do for Wild and Wonderful and the team. She was no longer needed in Egypt—not that she considered she'd been needed in the first place. Greg could handle everything until Jordan returned from Luxor and the two of them met with the Egyptian Ministry of Agriculture.

Oh, my God! Jordan! She wouldn't see Jordan before she left Egypt. Would she ever see him again? Did he assume, after all, that there was nothing between them? Other than one memorable night of making love, leaving her afraid to commit to a relationship she couldn't see lasting past the Egyptian border? So much for her magic carpet ride—her great adventure—she'd give the genie lamp to Lindsey. It hadn't done her much good so far anyway.

Pulling herself together, she made the necessary arrangements, freshened up, and then went to meet Greg for a lunch she had no stomach for at the moment.

Greg opened his door before Megan could knock.

"I was just coming to get you." Greg's smile dropped the minute he looked at her tear-stained face. "Hey, what's wrong?"

Gad, she was a mess—her eyes were sore, and she was pretty sure they were red, despite the cool compresses she'd applied, along with fresh makeup. She wiped at her eyes before answering.

"Bad news from home," Megan's voice wobbled. "My Mom had another stroke and isn't doing well. I need to go home. I've already called and made the arrangements. I'm sorry to leave you and Jordan in the lurch like this, but I'm all the family my mother has, and I want to be by her side."

"Not to worry. What time is your flight?"

"This afternoon. I've already packed and arranged for a taxi."

"Do you have time for lunch before you go?"

"I want to get back to the airport and check in. I'll pick up something there. Thanks for all your help, Greg. You've made my travels in Egypt much easier."

"If you need any references for Wild and Wonderful, give me a call. I'd be glad to write you a letter of recommendation."

"That's very kind of you. Thanks."

Although Greg's recommendation might be useful, she was sure Jordan's was the one that really counted. After her behavior the last couple of days, she wasn't so sure it would be forthcoming. He had enough on his plate to worry about without thinking about her and her job.

Her mind buzzed as she went back to her room to retrieve her luggage and wait for the taxi in the hotel lobby. She was anxious to get home to her mother, but she wasn't happy about leaving Cairo without talking to Jordan first. If for no other reason than to make sure he and his family were no longer in danger.

Megan checked out at reception, found a seat in the lobby next to the exit, and waited for the taxi. Looking through the glass doors and floor to ceiling windows, she watched the Nile rush by on the other side of the street. River boats docked, feluccas set sail, people walked along the boardwalk, and vendors sold their wares. A lot had happened since coming to Egypt with Jordan. She was sorry to have to cut her time short—there was so much more she'd like to have discovered. Jordan and his father had put dreams of possibilities in her head, places to explore, adventures to be had. And Jordan—Jordan had stolen her heart, and she had been stupid enough to walk away.

"So, I hear you're headed home."

Megan looked up to find Whitney standing over her, a wicked smirk on her otherwise perfect face, tanned from the Egyptian sun. And as usual she was dressed to kill.

"Unfortunately, my mother has had another stroke."

"I'm sorry. But don't worry, I'll take good care of Jordan for you," Whitney cooed, her sly smile an indication of her true intent.

"I know what you're planning, Whitney. Haven't you done enough damage already?" Megan stood and faced her adversary. Apparently, Whitney had taken an earlier flight as well and returned to Cairo ahead of the other conference attendees. "Why don't you just leave well enough alone? Other than vying for the same contract, why ruin Jordan's entire career? Are you that bitter?"

"Oh, Megan, such a novice. Go on home and take care of your mother and leave Jordan to me. You do realize he's been playing with you just to show me up—again. It doesn't mean anything. You don't mean anything to him. Men like him know how to play the game. Those innocent eyes of yours are a red flag waving in front of a love-starved man. He's out of your league."

"You're wrong about Jordan. He's not in love with you."

Megan gathered her luggage and made her way to the door to wait, leaving Whitney standing with a self-satisfied smirk and knowing raised eyebrow. The doorman opened the door and Megan stepped into the hot afternoon. But not before Whitney's taunting remarks followed her out into the bright Cairo sunshine.

"Who said anything about love?"

****

Jordan returned to the hotel in Luxor only to learn that there had been another accident. This one more serious.

"Omar was found dead, along with two other men the authorities said were members of the smuggling ring they had been investigating," Salah said.

"Omar? Are they sure he wasn't trying to stop the smugglers?" Jordan couldn't believe Omar had been implicated. He was a staunch member of his father's team.

"Sorry, no. We have been trailing him for some time. He had the missing artifacts in his possession. He, along with the others, was in the process of shipping them out. A gun fight with the authorities resulted."

"My father will be devastated to hear this."

"I am sorry I was not able to share this information sooner, as the investigation was still on-going. They are looking for Habib El-Said now."

"I'm not familiar with him. Do you think my father is in danger?"

"I would hope not, but Habib had ties with Omar, and fortunately your Ms. Holloway had taken pictures while at your father's dig the other day and had taken some of Habib talking to Omar. They happened to be exchanging an artifact. I am sorry, Jordan, I know he was your father's friend, but as you can see, he used his friendship for his own means."

"Then my father is in danger. Excuse me, while I return to warn him."

"I assure you the authorities are already on their way. Come. I will take you there."

Jordan didn't question how Salah knew all this, but he wasn't questioning anything right now. He had to return to the site to make sure his father was not in harm's way."

Jordan jumped from the vehicle as soon as Salah drew to a halt at Jordan's father's excavation site. Archeologists huddled in a group at the edge of the dig, facing the tent that was surrounded by police. His father stood in the center under the canopy. Habib El-Said faced him, gun in hand. Jordan raced forward. The police stopped him short of entering the tent.

"That's my father," Jordan stated. "What in hell is going on here?"

"You Kaines. You think you can come to Egypt and walk off with our priceless artifacts." Habib's loud angry voice vibrated in the arid desert air. "You think to take over our agriculture, run our economy—tell us how to run things like we are some kind of stupid."

"We are not walking off with your precious artifacts," his father returned. "It is not our decision to make. We are funded by various historic organizations, including the Egyptian Antiquities Ministry. My son is working with your Ministry of Agriculture. If you had done your research, you would know that. He is here to work with your farmers to improve their crops in order to feed your people, not ours."

Proud of his father for standing up to Habib El-Said, regardless of whether or not a gun was aimed at his chest, Jordan stepped forward. But before he could go two feet, a commotion ensued and a gunshot echoed across the desert. Police rushed under the canopy, cuffed Habib, and dragged him toward their vehicle.

Jordan's father lay on the desert sand, eyes closed. Jordan ran to his side, heart racing. Was he too late? Had Habib killed his father?

"Dad? Dad?" Jorden knelt beside him, his heart pounding in his chest. Wanting to touch him, shake him, to make sure he was all right, he didn't dare in case he caused more damage.

"Son," Henry Kaine said, opening his eyes. "I'm fine. I'm not hurt."

Jordan shot to his feet at the sound of his father's voice. Thank God, he hadn't been killed.

"Are you sure you're okay? I saw him shoot you, heard the gunshot."

"Yes, I'm sure. I would know if I'd been hit." His father sat up as if nothing had happened. He stood and smiled at everyone. "Except for my bum hitting the hard sand, thanks to Salah tripping me with his foot and knocking me over in time. I am still alive. He saved my life."

Jordan shook his head, stunned at the turn of events, relieved that his father hadn't been killed. He hugged his father, patted him on his back. "Don't ever do that to me again. You scared the living daylights out of me."

"It wasn't the best moment of my life, either, son." Jordan's father hugged him, and then turned to the man standing next to him.

Salah Delagad. When had he come forward?

"Thank you for saving my father's life." Jordan stepped forward to shake Salah's hand.

Salah Delagad reciprocated, and smiled.

"My pleasure. Good to see you have not come to harm, my friend." He turned to Jordan's father. "Many apologies for keeping you in the dark, as they say."

Salah pivoted to encompass the authorities who remained close by and nodded his thanks. "I have been working undercover with the authorities to break the smuggling ring. Thanks to your Ms. Holloway, she was able to provide pictures of Omar's meeting with Habib, who held in his hand one of the items found at your dig. Omar is dead, by the way, thanks to Habib's orders."

"What? What about Caleb?" his father asked. "Is my son safe?"

"Your son is safe and will be released as soon as you make arrangements to go pick him up from hospital."

"I assume it is now permissible for me to leave Luxor and return to my conference in Cairo?" Jordan asked, anxious to make sure Megan and the others were safe.

"We will need you to remain a bit longer in case we have question," Salah said. "But I assure you, I will put in a good word for you and your colleagues. I hear they have safely returned to Cairo."

Jordan had to hand it to Megan. If she hadn't questioned Omar's involvement at the conference and his sudden association with Whitney and connecting him with the man she had seen at his father's dig, the authorities might not have had proof so soon of Habib El-Said's connection. He couldn't wait to see her, tell her how her pictures had helped solve the case, tell her how much she meant to him.

Now if she would only give him a chance to explain how much he cared for her. Dare he say love her? Yes. Dammit. He loved her.

Damn the contracts. Damn tenure.

He couldn't wait to return to Cairo and find Megan—tell her he loved her. Make her listen this time.

Chapter Fourteen

"Where's Megan?" Jordan asked Greg the minute his coworker answered the door.

"Don't you mean how are the contracts going?" Greg asked with a smirk.

Jordan wanted to wipe the grin off Greg's know-it-all face.

"You're right. Then I want to know where Megan is. She isn't answering her door."

"The Ministry of Agriculture accepted our proposal with a caveat."

"Great. Good to know. Now where the hell is Megan?"

"She flew back to New York yesterday. You're a day late."

"What? What do you mean she flew back to New York yesterday? What's going on?"

"Come on in and get out of the hallway and we'll talk. Or maybe you'd like to go to the bar and get a drink."

"No drink. Although it's sounding more and more like I need one."

Jordan followed Greg into the suite, plunked down in the easy chair next to the balcony window, and sighed. Megan had left, dammit. He was too late.

"Okay, so, Megan's mother had another stroke, so she had to leave. There is nothing you can do at the moment except concentrate on the reason we're here in the first place. Get a grip, man," Greg said. "As for the meeting with the Ministry of Agriculture's team, the information you gave me helped seal the deal."

"Great. Then there is nothing more I need to do here," Jordan said, still not focusing on their proposal. Ready to bolt out the door to do what? Shit. He was too late. And he wasn't due to leave Cairo for two more days.

"Earth to Jordan, earth to Jordan. Have you not heard what I'm trying to tell you?"

"Okay, what am I missing?" Jordan sat forward, arms dangling over knees waiting for Greg to continue.

"I told you there was a caveat. They want another meeting."

"Why? What's the stipulation?"

"They want us to collaborate with Dr. Norland from Florida. They feel his proposal and ours complements each other, a better diverse yet complete comprehensive program that would also be easy to implement."

"Are you agreeable to this?" Jordan's mind now fully engaged in the project, he wanted particulars.

"I've listened to Dr. Norland, and I agree. The meeting is to work out the kinks, funding, and collaborating team members. It sounds like a win-win for everyone involved."

"I need to make a few phone calls, get some lunch, then we can sit down and go over the details before the meeting. When is it scheduled?"

"We have plenty of time. Make your calls, then I'll join you for lunch. Say, in an hour?"

Jordan checked his watch. "Should be plenty of time. I'll meet you in the café down the street."

****

Lindsey was waiting for Megan in the luggage claim area in Ithaca when she walked through the doors. Her friend greeted her with a warm welcoming, yet sympathetic hug.

"I'm so sorry about your mom, Megan," Lindsey said. "It must have been an awful flight worrying about her without any further news. Did you get any sleep?"

"Not a wink. So, fill me in. How is she?" Megan ignored the luggage circling the turnstile, anxious to find out about her mother. "Is she still in the hospital? Is she going to be okay?"

"Yes. As soon as we get your things I'll get you home so you can go see her. But she's doing okay, so try to relax. I've been told she lost the use of one arm, and it affected her left eye. They'll know more in a couple of days."

"Thanks so much for being there for her, Lindsey. It made my job in Egypt much easier to do. Not that it was hard. In fact, I felt like a tourist most of the time."

"We have plenty of time on the drive home so you can fill me in. Let's get your bags and get out of here. I'm dying to hear all about your adventures with Jordan Kaine. Remember, you promised me a blow by blow account."

"You asked for an account, I didn't say I was going to give you one. Oh, look, there's my luggage."

Lindsey laughed as Megan rushed to the turnstile to retrieve her suitcase. There was no way she was going to tell Lindsey about her one-night stand with Jordan. No way. Her adventures along the Nile were another matter. The experiences she'd had a chance to take part in were going to be hard not to talk about—they were etched in her memory for all time.

"I hope you have something warmer to wear than that gauzy thing you have on. Did you forget its December—as in cold, snowy weather?"

"My jacket is in my carry on. Give me a minute to get it out." Moving out of the way of others retrieving their belongings, Megan quickly slipped into her teal jacket and zipped it up. She was glad Lindsey reminded her to put it on, as once they stepped outside and crossed over to the parking area, the cold winter blustery wind coming off Cayuga Lake made it hard to hang on to her suitcases.

Once they were on the road, Lindsey started in on her.

"So, Jordan Kaine. How'd that go?"

"The conference was interesting. Glad I had a chance to be part of another country's culture. I learned a lot about farming methods on a more basic level. I don't know if Jordan and Greg will win the contract, but after collaborating with Greg yesterday, I feel we have a good chance. I just hope my coming home two days early doesn't hurt their chances—or my job."

"Glad to know about your work, but that isn't what I meant and you know it. I have no doubts you'll get the contract. What I want to know is more personal—you and Jordan Kaine. How did that go? Especially after you mentioned that Whitney Nash showed up. Don't tell me she put a monkey-wrench in the whole affair?"

Lindsey didn't know how close to the truth she was by mentioning an affair. But Megan wasn't going there.

"There were several accidents, most of which centered on Jordan's father's archaeological dig outside Luxor."

"Wait. What? You experienced an actual dig? Even I haven't done that! I'm envious."

"It was awesome. However, as I said, a few accidents occurred, including finding a dead body on one of our field trips."

"What?"

Megan proceeded to fill Lindsey in on all the mishaps including the incident with the hot air balloon excursion. She left out the carriage ride with Jordan and their night spent in each other's arms. Lindsey would have a field day with that one, and right now, she was too vulnerable to discuss it. She was sure Whitney was at this very moment trying to wrap herself around Jordan. She didn't even want to contemplate the outcome.

"I know you're keeping something from me, Megan. What aren't you telling me?"

"If you don't lay off, *girlfriend*, I'm not going to give you the genie lamp I brought you," Megan said as Lindsey drove her car into the driveway in front of Megan's home.

"OMG! A genie lamp! Just what I need—three wishes." Lindsey laughed. "Can't wait to give it a try. How about you? Did you buy one for yourself?"

Megan wasn't about to tell Lindsey that Jordan had bought one for her. It was too personal and tucked away in her suitcase out of sight.

"No. I found this one in a spice bazaar and couldn't resist. Thought you'd be able to use it to find your own true love."

"Maybe we should both make a wish on it."

"Nope. It's yours," Megan said stepping from the car. "Good luck."

"That's what a genie lamp is all about." Lindsey smiled.

Megan waved Lindsey off, dragged her luggage down the sidewalk that someone had thoughtfully cleared for her, and entered the house. Her mother's dog greeted her.

"Hello, Abby." The dog wagged her tail and then rushed forward to nuzzle Megan's neck. "Good to see you, too, girl," Megan said, kneeling to rub behind the dog's ears. After making sure the dog was settled, Megan quickly freshened up, grabbed her car keys, a heavier coat and boots, and then drove to the hospital to visit her mother. She found a spot in the hospital parking lot, turned the ignition off, and took a deep breath. Trying to remain lighthearted with Lindsey had relieved some of the stress during their ride from the airport. Now it was time to face whatever waited for her here at the hospital. Hopefully Lindsey was right, and her mother was going to be okay.

But after seeing her mother propped up in her hospital bed, eyes shut, IV and a myriad of tubes attached to her arms, Megan wasn't so sure her mother was going to be okay. Megan's heart sank as she stepped closer, not wanting to disturb her mother, but wanting her mother to know that she had returned from Egypt. She laid a hand on her mother's frail hand. Surprisingly strong fingers gripped Megan's hand and tightened, then loosened. Her mother's eyes opened— she emitted a soft sigh. Tears gathered and fell on to pale cheeks. Megan leaned forward and kissed her mother's forehead, then searched for a tissue to wipe her mother's tears away.

"I won't leave you again," Megan promised. "I'm here to take care of you. We'll get through this together." Job or no job, there was no way she was going to leave her mother's side until she was well on the mend this time.

Megan's mother sniffled. Her wobbly lips curved upward. "Love you." Her whispered words trembled.

"Love you, too, Mom. Now just relax and get well. I'm not going anywhere until we get this worked out." Megan pulled a chair next to the bed, held her mother's hand, and sat until her mother's eyes closed, her breathing evened, and her hand grew limp.

Megan quietly rose and left the room in search of the doctor. It was time to get help in dealing with her mother's current condition—it obviously wasn't going to be a quick recovery. And one she wasn't going to be able to handle on her own. And she couldn't even think about getting a positive recommendation and keeping her job after walking out on Jordan. Besides, how could she work on the project with him after all they had shared, should they be awarded the contract? The best thing to do would be to simply look for another job come Monday.

Monday found Megan making arrangements for her mother to be admitted to a permanent senior assisted-living facility. With her mother losing the use of her left arm, and the sight in the left eye, she had finally agreed that this type of arrangement was best. A huge turnaround from the normal guilt trips her mother was accustomed to dishing out. Once Nettie learned that her doctors and the hospital staff recommended a facility that had an active life-style living center, as well as a physical therapy program, and that she would be able to participate in a number of activities on a daily basis, as well as practically have the run of the place, her mother agreed. After a few more days in the hospital, if she continued to improve, her mother would be transferred to the prestigious facility overlooking Cayuga Lake.

After another stressful day making the arrangements for her mother's health care, and working with the insurance adjustors, Megan stopped by for carry-out at one of the local Thai restaurants, and then drove home to figure out her next move. Tomorrow she'd face Wild and Wonderful, turn in her report, and hope she still had a job. In the meantime, she decided to download the pictures she'd taken in Egypt onto her laptop in preparation for her final report to Helen.

Megan set up her laptop on the living room coffee table and downloaded her pictures. She scanned them as they were processing, her mind on the report, when the picture of her and Jordan standing in front of the Sphinx popped up on the screen. Her heart skipped a beat. She paused the screen and stared at the two of them, arms wrapped around each other—a reminder of their adventures—a real romantic fantasy come to life—and wondered at what might have been. She let the pictures finish downloading and shut the computer off.

The dog barked as it sat next to the front door waiting to go for a walk. After being in Egypt's hot climate the past week and a half, she was feeling the cold winter weather, so taking Abby for a walk before it got dark wasn't something she was looking forward to.

"Okay, girl. We'll just take a short walk around the block, but then we're hunkering down for the night."

Abby wagged her tail, waited patiently while Megan dressed in her outerwear, and grabbed the dog leash. A cold blast of winter air hit her head on. It was going to be a shorter walk than normal. Abby didn't hesitate either and within ten minutes they were back inside. Megan settled in the sitting room with a cup of hot tea with lemon and honey. Alone, her mind wandered back to her wonderful adventures in Egypt. Adventures that she'd remember for the rest of her life, thanks to Jordan. Despite the misfortune that had befallen his father and the conference, she smiled, recalling the emotions that had filled her entire being while riding a camel with Jordan sitting behind her. Visiting the pyramids, the Sphinx, the Nile, and the balloon ride. Oh, Lord, the carriage ride—and making love.

She glanced at the genie lamp she'd placed on the coffee table that morning. She clasped it in her hands, rubbed her palms over each side, wishing it really worked, and that Jordan really loved her, and that it hadn't been a one-night stand, like Whitney had implied. She hugged the lamp to her chest, sighed, and replaced it on the table. About to go to the kitchen to refill her teacup, the doorbell rang. She'd remembered Lindsey had promised to stop by later to drop off Abby's play toys she'd left behind.

Megan opened the door and gasped.

"Jordan!" Megan stepped back, shocked as if she'd conjured him up for real. "What are you doing here?"

Jordan didn't wait to be invited in. Instead, he stepped inside, shut the door, enfolded her in his arms and kissed her speechless. She didn't resist. She clung to him as if he would vanish any second. Oh, my God, it was like being held in his embrace back in Egypt. The sensations coursed through her until her legs gave out. Thankfully, Jordan had a tight hold on her. He lifted her with ease and carried her to the sofa.

"I was devastated when I learned you had left Cairo before we could work things out. I wanted to tell you how much making love to you meant to me. I was hoping you felt the same."

"It was all happening too fast. I had so much on my plate here at home. I didn't want you to have to deal with my baggage. It's not your burden to bear."

"I thought you were concerned about my reputation and didn't want to be associated with me. Especially after we made love. Figured you considered all those accusations about me were true. It didn't help when Whitney showed up and tried to cause trouble between us, as well as over the contracts with the Egyptian government."

"Oh, Jordan, I knew better. I've known what Whitney was like and was confident you weren't to blame. But I was concerned that any relationship with you on this trip might hurt your chances of getting tenure. I didn't want to be the cause of that. And if I know Whitney, she would try to cause trouble for you in that regard."

"I wouldn't worry about Whitney at this point. I heard her job is in jeopardy after trying to sway the Egyptian Ministry of Agriculture, as well as her connections with Omar, which didn't garner her any brownie points. Besides, if I have to decide between our relationship and tenure, I'll forego tenure. You mean much more to me, Megan. I love you. I don't want to lose you."

Tears of happiness misted in Megan's eyes. Did he really just say he loved her?

"Oh, Jordan. I've had such a crush on you since I was in your class." She let the tears fall, raised her face to his. "I don't want to be the reason you don't get tenure and ruin your career. After everything you've been through with Whitney, I don't want our relationship to ruin something you've worked so hard for."

"Hush. If my peers at the university think the worst of me because of my love for you, then it's not the place for me."

"I love you, too."

Jordan gathered her in his arms again and kissed her—a kiss that made all her worries vanish in a heartbeat.

"Confession time." Jordan smiled, as they leaned back on the sofa still wrapped in each other's arms. "I had a crush on you, too. But I knew better than to act on it. And after the Whitney debacle, I didn't want to get involved with anyone for a long time, especially one of my students. But seeing you that day at the office and learning that you were assigned to accompany me to Egypt, I was torn between having to deal with a novice, and ecstatic that you were the one that would be traveling with me."

"I was so worried about my performance review, and making a good impression," Megan said, "that I was torn between making sure I didn't mess up, and wanting to be with you, too."

"Trust me, after you helped the authorities identify Omar with Habib El-Said, by turning over your photos, your performance review is in the bag. Not to mention the exceptional performance the night we spent together. I was heartbroken when you left my side and later wouldn't talk about it the next morning."

"Actually, your performance wasn't so bad either. In fact, I kicked myself for being such a jerk for not discussing it the next day. I thought I blew it. And then when I was called home, and Whitney threw a few accusations my way as I was leaving, I was sure I'd never see you again. And that I'd lose my job."

"Well, you haven't lost your job. To the contrary, we will be working closely together with Dr. Norland and his team from Florida on the Egyptian project."

"That's wonderful. You and Greg got the contract?"

"*We* got the contract—in conjunction with Dr. Norland. Which means *we* will be spending a lot of time in Egypt over the next few years. We never did get to visit the Valley of the Kings. It'll be our first stop. Do you think you can handle it?"

"Me?"

"Yes. You're part of the team."

It was all Megan could do not to jump for joy. She'd fallen in love with Egypt. She had fallen in love with Jordan. If he was by her side, she could only imagine the new adventures they could share.

"There is one stipulation," Jordan said, his hands circling her cheeks, his eyes mesmerizing her.

"What?" Megan whispered, her heart racing, waiting, hoping for him to say the words she longed to hear. She held her breath.

"Will you marry me?"

Megan closed her eyes, leaned in, kissed him, and paused only long enough to answer "yes."

No words were necessary as the night closed in around them—and the genie lamp, now forgotten in the center of the coffee table, emitted a warm sensual glow.

A word about the author…

Carol Henry is an award winning and #1 Amazon Best Selling author who writes contemporary romance, as well as Destination: Romance—Exotic, Romantic Suspense Adventures. Carol lives with her husband in the beautiful New York State Finger Lakes area where they are surrounded by family, friends, and wildlife. World travelers, Carol writes about her international adventures for major cruise lines' deluxe in-cabin books and magazines and takes pleasure in sharing her adventures with her readers in her 'Connection' series. A local NYS historian, Carol has written several books on her town's history.

For more information visit her website at: http://www.carolhenry.org

~*~

Other Carol Henry titles
available from The Wild Rose Press, Inc.:

Amazon Connection
Breakfast with Santa
Dare to Run
Juelle's Legacy
Nothing Short of a Miracle
Ribbons of Steel
Rio Connection
Shanghai Connection

www.ingramcontent.com/pod-product-compliance
Lightning Source LLC
Chambersburg PA
CBHW060931180626
46817CB00004B/1484